VALLEY OF FIRE

By the Author

All Things Rise

The Ground Beneath

The Time Before Now

Whiskey Sunrise

Valley of Fire

Writing as Paige Braddock

Jane's World: The Case of the Mail Order Bride

VALLEY OF FIRE

by
Missouri Vaun

2016

ISBN 13: 978-1-62639-496-4

This Trade Paperback Original Is Published By
Bold Strokes Books, Inc.
P.O. Box 249
Valley Falls, NY 12185

First Edition: October 2016

CREDITS
Editor: Cindy Cresap
Production Design: Susan Ramundo
Cover Design By Sheri (graphicartist2020@hotmail.com)
Character Art By Paige Braddock
Background Painting By Elizabeth Leggett

Acknowledgments

Ava, who first appeared in *All Things Rise*, finally gets her own story in *Valley of Fire*. Almost as soon as I'd finished *All Things Rise*, I had Ava's story in mind, but it took this long to get the story in print.

First, I had to run my story by Cris, a chemist friend of mine, to see if my ideas were plausible. This involved conversations about genetically modified food and the components of plants and how pathogens work. Thank you, Cris. I couldn't have written this story without your help.

I'd also like to acknowledge the stellar crew at Bold Strokes Books. I'm very grateful to Rad, Sandy, Ruth, Sheri, and especially my editor Cindy for making this book a reality.

As many other writers know, beta readers are an integral part of the process. I'd like to thank D. Jackson Leigh, Alena, Jenny, and Vanessa for all your notes and feedback about this story. Thank you, thank you, thank you.

Special thanks to my wife Evelyn for love and support and for allowing me to hide in my studio and write late into the night without complaint. And thanks to my great-grandmother, Missouri Vaun, for letting me use her name.

Dedication

To my wife, Evelyn, for a great book title.

CHAPTER ONE

A ribbon of white sandy coastline stretched north, growing narrower as it intersected the thin blue horizon. The slightest halo of pink warmed the sky just at the earth's edge signaling the approaching sunset. Ava banked the aircraft and headed out over the open sea toward the cloud city of Easton.

When Ava Wynne met high-speed proton fusion propulsion, it was love at first sight. She could still remember the first time she'd flown as a test pilot. She'd felt vulnerable and exposed as she sat beneath the curved glass covering the cockpit, yet in control at the same time. With each maneuver, as she climbed or banked, gravity's pull against the torque of the engines pressed her body into the seat. Adrenaline surged through her system, and she had to remind herself to breathe. Being a pilot might be the only thing she truly loved with enthusiasm and without reservation.

And she'd never yearned for more, until recently. Restlessness cast in front of her like a lengthy late afternoon shadow. Something was missing from her life. If only she could figure out what that something was.

A monotone voice from CC Easton's flight tower came through her headset giving the cargo craft clearance to land. Ava reached over and flipped a series of switches, initiating the landing sequence. In the seat beside her, Jenna Bookman spoke to the tower as she took command of the aircraft's approach and descent. Within minutes, they would be easing into a wide hangar on the flight deck. They made their approach from the southeast, circling the enormous city center hovering above the clouds. Sunlight danced across the glass skyscrapers of the central quadrant as they flew past.

Flashing lights in the entry tunnel matched their speed until the aircraft's forward motion stopped. Deck crews gathered behind protective barriers as the cargo ship hovered above its assigned landing grid.

Jenna spoke to the tower again as she lowered the craft to the flight deck and powered down. Ava loved takeoff and navigation; she was happy to let Jenna handle the reentry and shutdown. The engine's hum lulled and then was silent as Jenna powered down.

"It's not too late to change your mind, you know." Jenna removed her headset and looked at Ava.

"I'm not going to change my mind. You can always come visit me." Ava had flown with Jenna for a long time, but today was their last flight together. Ava had requested a transfer to the cloud city of San Francisco, and the transfer had been approved. She hoped the move would settle her feelings of restlessness. Maybe a new city was all she needed.

"Right. You'll be in a new city with a fresh dating pool. You'll have no time for your old married friends."

"Jenna Bookman, you are anything but old and you're barely married. I'll always have time for you." Ava smiled at Jenna and playfully punched her shoulder.

"What are you up to for your last night in Easton?"

"I'm meeting Sara out." Ava gathered her gear bag and headed toward the side exit just behind the cockpit. She walked past large containers labeled SYN/BIO as she exited the cargo bay door and was reminded that someone would have to stay until the containers were signed for and removed.

"Well, you ladies have fun." Jenna leaned through the door.

Ava turned back for a minute. "Hey, I can stay until someone signs for those."

"No way. Get outta here. Go be young. Make bad choices. I've got this." Jenna waved her off.

Ava hesitated. She thought maybe she should say something, but she and Jenna had never been much for sentimental talk, and she knew their paths would cross in one city or another given the constant travel they both did. So it wasn't like this was good-bye, it was more like good-bye for now. "Thanks. I'll see you around."

"Make me proud out there on the West Coast, okay?" Jenna leaned through the narrow side door of the cargo bay, resting an elbow on each side. Ava took a mental picture of the scene. She knew this was one of those moments she'd reflect back on as a big transition that she'd played off as small. Jenna had been her mentor and her friend.

Fuck it. Ava walked back, climbed the few steps from the tarmac, and pulled her into a hug. "Thanks for everything, Jen."

"My pleasure, kid." Jenna held on to her for a minute longer than she needed to.

Ava smiled and waved over her shoulder as she left and headed toward her residential cube. She had a few hours of down time before she was supposed to meet Sara. She'd shower and get some food. Ava wanted her last night in CC Easton to be a good one, and if all went well, she wouldn't spend it alone. She searched her comm unit for Sara's number and waited for her to answer.

Flanked by two security officers, Leland passed through the main gate and walked toward the cargo ship that had just settled into hangar bay six. The tarmac was busy with foot traffic and small maglev carriers hauling cargo from one point to another.

Through the hum of activity, Leland became suddenly aware of one person in particular. A woman in a flight suit strode confidently toward her. As she drew closer, Leland was taken by her fair complexion, classic square jawline, and dark hair pulled back into a knot at her nape. Even wearing the flight suit, her feminine, yet firm, athletic build was obvious. The tight fitting suit hugged every slight curve, and Leland found it difficult not to stare. The woman was speaking into her comm device and only briefly glanced in Leland's direction as she passed by.

Leland couldn't resist turning to watch the woman's retreating figure. She tried to make the backward glance quick, but a murmured remark from one of the security escorts told her she'd been caught looking.

"Were you saying something?" asked Leland.

"Sorry, nothing." The guard stifled a cough, as if he was trying not to laugh.

It didn't matter anyway. Women rarely caught Leland's attention. Even if they did, she never got the chance to follow up. There was always too much work to do, and when there wasn't, there were family obligations that kept her from having the freedom to pursue her own desires.

They reached the cargo hold and entered through the small side door. The containers she'd come for were right up front. Leland didn't usually claim the materials personally, but she was the only individual from the lab with a high enough security clearance not quarantined with the flu. She'd been wondering if an official statement was forthcoming from the World Health Organization because she was worried that this particular virus was getting very close to pandemic status. Anyone who had any sort of access to that level of information seemed to be very tight-lipped. Even her father, and she'd asked him directly.

Leland stepped into the cargo bay. "Hello, I'm here to sign for this shipment."

A woman in a flight suit similar to the one she'd just seen moved around the containers and handed her a digital tablet. The woman seemed older than the other female pilot she'd just seen, seasoned, with more of a square build and short dark hair that touched her collar. "I'm Jenna Bookman. I was told to wait with the materials until someone signed for them. Can I just get a thumbprint here?"

Leland accepted the tablet Jenna offered and held her thumb to the screen for a few seconds. The screen flashed green and Jenna nodded. "Okay, you're good to go."

The two security guards loaded four containers onto a small carrier that hovered about three feet off the ground at the foot of the stairs, just beside the aircraft's cargo door. Within minutes, the containers were loaded and the three of them began their trek back across the tarmac.

A half hour later, Leland had the containers in the lab and was systematically checking the plant materials each carried. She would test the samples for pathogens. Organic herbs had their own natural bacteria, but she was checking for the ones that would be harmful if ingested.

Leland placed specimens from each container on Petri slides. She'd feed them, put them in a warm safe place, and come back tomorrow to see what was growing. She mixed a solution and then a series of dilutions that Leland placed on Petrifilm. She slid the tray of samples into the incubator and closed the front shield.

She sighed and sank back onto a stool near the center counter that split the sterile space in two halves. It was late and she was the only one left in the lab. Left alone, Leland was having thoughts that she didn't want to have. Thoughts that she'd been trying to ignore. She didn't want to know certain things because once she knew them she couldn't un-know them. She rubbed her eyes and pinched the space between them. The shadow of a headache was hovering, and she wanted to ward it off.

Leland thought most people were sheep. Lucky sheep that were allowed, encouraged even, to be blissfully unaware of the dark matter that made the world run. Not for the first time, she wished she were a sheep. So that she could forget that she knew things. That kind of forgetting might require assistance.

She scrubbed her hands, paused in the detox chamber, and then signed out for the night. She pulled on a jacket as she stepped outside. It was dark and the temp was dropping. The glass-sided buildings surrounding the pedestrian corridor were aglow with light against the night sky. She must have been in the lab longer than she'd intended. Her driver stepped out and opened the rear door of the small transport for her. Two other figures in dark clothing seemed to come alive when she exited the building. They waited beside their vehicle as she approached the forward car.

Leland hesitated. She should just go to the hotel and get some sleep, but she really didn't want to think about her research for a few hours, and she knew if she went to the hotel that's all she'd do. She'd lie in bed and stare at the ceiling while data ran in a recurring loop through her tired brain.

"Is something wrong?" the young man dressed all in black asked her as he held the door open.

"I was thinking I might go out."

"Out?"

"For a drink."

"Oh." He looked at her like she'd just said the craziest thing he'd ever heard.

"I know I don't usually do that, but if I were to do that sort of thing do you have any suggestions?"

"Sure. I can think of a couple of spots."

"Just take me to the nearest one, okay?"

"Absolutely."

Leland climbed in and sank into the seat as the driver accelerated away from the curb. Lights from the second car, now trailing them, illuminated the interior. Within minutes, he slowed and veered. He opened the glass between the compartments. "This is the most popular nightclub. If you don't like what you see we can go to a different place."

"I'm sure this will be fine."

He climbed out and opened the door for her. "I'll wait here for you, ma'am."

"I wish you'd just call me Leland."

"Yes, ma'am."

"Okay, forget it. I'll see you shortly." Leland walked toward the sound of thumping dance music. The silver and glass, multistory structure had different colored neon at each level that seemed to pulse with the beat of the music throbbing from the main entrance. She nodded in the direction of her ever-present shadow detail. They followed her inside at a respectable distance.

Leland couldn't remember the last time she'd gone into a club, in public. But this was a city where no one knew her. Anonymity felt like a small taste of freedom. She breathed it in as she stepped into the crowded first floor of the nightclub.

CHAPTER TWO

Ava spotted Sara at a tall table near the back of the club with her newest romantic lead just after she arrived. Ava liked Sara's newest fling. Kelly was cute, fun, a great dancer, and most importantly, apolitical. Kelly was just what Sara needed. Sara's last love interest had gotten her involved with an underground political movement that managed to plant several bombs in strategic sites that almost brought Easton to its knees. The Return to Earth movement had almost caused CC Easton's complete collapse. Sara was still laboring under the guilt she felt for believing that the insurgency's leader, Meredith, had only nonviolent tactics planned. Meredith had not been captured, and so far had managed to elude authorities. Poor Sara. Her idealism had suffered a fatal blow.

Yeah, Kelly was just what Sara needed. Cute, sweet, shallow.

Ava downed half of Sara's cocktail and tugged them toward the dance floor. After a few songs, they returned to the table and actually managed to get a waitress to bring them drinks.

"It's only because you're here. They always ignore me." Sara leaned over to practically yell in Ava's direction.

"I don't believe you."

"Believe it," Kelly chimed in. "You're hot and you're getting us noticed, thank you! You can drink with us any time."

"Don't tell her that. She knows she's hot. Don't inflate her ego even more."

Then Sara looked sad, and Ava shook her head. "No, don't do that. We're not going to turn tonight into some big sad thing. We're here to have fun, remember?" Sara nodded. Ava knew she'd miss her friends in Easton, but she was excited about the possibilities she'd find in CC San Francisco. And besides, she'd have Easton on her flight schedule from time to time. She was sure of it. "So, who should I ask to dance?"

Sara and Ava frequently played this matchup game at the club. They would take turns picking out women for each other. The goal was to make the target a challenge, so they usually picked against type.

Kelly drew Sara close. "Oh no, not tonight. Sara's out of play tonight. This evening she's all mine." She pulled Sara into a kiss.

"Okay, okay, enough with the kissing." Ava smiled at them and sipped her drink.

"I've already picked someone out for you. As a matter of fact, I've seen her look over here at you a couple of times." Sara grinned as if she had some big secret to share.

"Who?" Ava tried to follow Sara's gaze.

"Over there. Short hair, dark glasses, gray jacket." Sara took Ava by the shoulders and turned her so that she was facing in the right direction. "There, she just looked over here again."

"She's too butch for me. No, thanks."

"I don't think she's butch. I think she's just tall and slim. Do you have some sort of maximum height requirement that I don't know about?"

Ava almost choked on her drink from laughing. "No."

"Okay, then. She's my challenge for you tonight. Go." Sara playfully shoved Ava.

"Seriously?"

"At least get close enough to see if she's really as butch as you think. Or better yet, bring her over here and we'll decide for you." Kelly was sitting behind Sara and pulled her backward and kissed her neck.

"You guys are cute together." So maybe she would ask tall, dark, and androgynous to dance. She put her glass on the table. "Okay, save my drink. This might be a quick trip."

Ava cut across the dance floor, weaving between clusters of women and past couples who seemed to be in their own world, moving to their own rhythm. Her friend Kate captured her in a hug as she squeezed past.

"When do you leave for CCSF?" Kate asked.

"Tomorrow. I'll call you before I leave."

"You better." Kate released her to continue her pursuit.

When she looked up again, she'd lost sight of her intended conquest. Ava scanned the club and spotted her leaning against the bar at the corner of the dance floor. Ava slipped into the small open space next to her.

Her mark was intent on an exchange with the bartender, giving Ava a chance to study her from a much closer vantage point. Sara had been right; she was only slightly taller than Ava, with a slender build, but she was definitely not butch. Androgynous was a better description, but decidedly feminine. She had short dark hair that looked intentionally shaped to look tousled. Ava thought it was intentional because the rest of the woman's attire sent a message of pure order. Her dark clothing had simple clean lines: a short waistcoat that covered an untucked shirt over dark slacks. Ava was quite distracted with her observations until she realized the woman had caught her looking down to check out her shoes.

"Hello."

"Sorry. I was just admiring your shoes."

"Really?"

Ava laughed. "No, not really." She held her hand out. "Hello, I'm Ava Wynne."

"Leland."

"Last name?"

"Um, James. Leland James."

"Did you have to think about that for a minute?" Ava couldn't see Leland's eyes behind the darkened glasses, but she felt the intensity of her gaze nonetheless. How was that possible?

"Can I buy you a drink?" Leland asked.

"How about if I buy you a drink?"

"My credits are already on the bar." Leland tapped her index finger on the card sitting on the bar's reflective surface near her glass.

"Okay then, bourbon. Neat."

They gathered their drinks and moved back to the table where Ava had seen Leland earlier. As they took seats across from each other, Ava couldn't help but notice how Leland's gray shirt hung open just enough to reveal the smooth skin of her elegant neck and a glimpse of her collarbone. Leland seemed a little nervous and ran her fingers through her hair, which did nothing to tame its unruly state. Ava thought she looked gorgeously unkempt. But she was puzzled about the dark glasses. Maybe the strobe lights bothered her.

"Do you come here often?" Leland asked.

Really? She must be nervous if that was the best she could do. "Yeah, fairly often. You?"

Leland shook her head. "I'm not from Easton."

Well, that explained why Ava hadn't seen Leland before, because she felt like she'd have noticed her. Although, Ava did have the weirdest feeling they'd met somewhere, briefly. Before she could give it much more thought, a song she liked began to play.

"Let's dance." Ava stood to move toward the floor.

Leland didn't respond and didn't move.

"Come on." Ava motioned for Leland to follow her. Once on the dance floor, Ava tried to study Leland without really studying her. Ava's approach to seduction was to remain aloof until she got some idea of whether she found a woman interesting enough to pursue more. And even after that discovery she sometimes remained aloof. Maybe protective was a better word. At any rate, this approach had worked well for her. Women seemed to love a challenge. Although, at the moment, Leland seemed as aloof as she was. If they both tried that approach, this would never move past a first dance.

Ava was normally drawn to women with more curves, but as she watched Leland move to the music, she was struck by how sexy she was. Pure sex appeal, thought Ava. *Hmm, interesting.* She wanted to change things up. Maybe she should start dating against type more often and see where that got her. Leland didn't feel incredibly confident on the dance floor. It had been a long time since she'd danced. And even longer since she'd danced with someone she found so attractive. She'd noticed Ava the minute she'd walked in. Leland recognized her from their brief encounter on the tarmac. She was fairly certain that Ava didn't remember seeing her.

Oh well, bruised ego aside, at least Ava had asked to buy her a drink. Now they'd have a dance and that would be the end of it. Leland resolved to have no investment in the outcome and simply enjoy Ava's company for as long as it lasted. She closed her eyes and swayed to the rhythmic beat as if she were alone, rather than in a room full of strangers. Beautiful strangers.

The sensation of someone touching her pulled her from her trance. She opened her eyes to see that Ava had moved much closer and was dancing against her with her hands on Leland's hips. If it was possible, Ava was even more stunning in close proximity. Her hair was down straight, and it hung just at her shoulders. She was wearing a low-cut dark knit shirt that clung to her upper body, revealing every subtle curve. The pants she wore fit like a second skin, only a few shades lighter in color than her shirt. The pants ended with heels that Leland reasoned took sheer athletic ability to dance in the way Ava was dancing in them.

Ava invaded her senses as she moved closer and placed a light kiss at the opening of her collar. To say Leland was surprised was an understatement. She'd assumed this was going nowhere, but the signals she was now receiving from Ava definitely gave her some glimmer of hope. She decided to test the waters.

Leland pulled Ava against her, insinuating her thigh between Ava's as they continued to move to the music. She closed her eyes again and gave herself over to the sensations of Ava's firm body moving against hers. She felt her system react as if a match had been struck. Heat flamed to her throat and face. She was relieved that the club was dark. Maybe Ava wouldn't notice how strongly Leland was reacting to the sensations of her.

How long had they been dancing, she wasn't sure. They were close now, Ava's arm was draped lightly across her shoulder, and Leland could feel the warmth from her skin as their faces were only inches apart. Tentatively, Leland brushed Ava's cheek with her lips. When Ava didn't pull away, she lightly kissed her on the mouth.

Ava's reaction was quick. She drew Leland into a deep kiss. Leland's heart pounded. Ava's touch was strong, sure, yet tender.

As the kiss ended, Ava reached to remove her dark glasses. "I need to see your eyes."

Leland shoved the shades into her jacket pocket and waited for what might happen next. After Ava studied her intently for a few seconds, she kissed Leland again lightly and pulled her toward the exit.

CHAPTER THREE

A va clasped Leland's hand and maneuvered through a small group of women entering the club. Once outside, she watched with curiosity as Leland replaced the dark glasses.

As they stepped out of the crowd at the front entrance, Ava noticed a young man dressed in black open the rear door of a waiting transport as if he knew them. After a moment, she realized he did know at least one of them.

Leland motioned toward the open door. "I have a car if you'd like to, um…if you'd like to go somewhere a bit more quiet."

"I'd like that." Ava climbed in first and settled into the seat facing Leland. The maglev transport, suspended over its metal track, sank only slightly as they climbed in. Now she was even more curious. What sort of person had a car service at their command?

As if anticipating the question, Leland began to speak. Her tone was calm, soothing. "When I travel, my work provides this service."

"Very considerate of them." Ava wondered what Leland's work was, but decided she didn't want to know too much. Sara always complained that Ava never asked enough questions, but this was a calculated tactic on Ava's part. The less she knew, the less she was accountable for. In this case, she was only planning one night at a time, especially since this was her last evening in CC Easton. So the less she knew, the better.

The driver spoke through the intercom system from the front of the luxury transport. "Where to, ma'am?"

Leland gave Ava a questioning look.

"Your place?" Ava didn't want to suggest her residential cube, which was currently filled with all of her belongings, boxed in transport crates for shipment to CCSF.

"The hotel, thanks." Leland settled back into the opposite seat.

The trip only took a few minutes. They'd hardly spoken on the ride. Ava was trying to decide how far she'd let the evening go. She hadn't even said good-bye to Sara, but she'd call her in the morning. That was the easiest way to avoid an emotional scene anyway. As they rode the lift, Ava noticed for the first time that Leland had pushed the button for the penthouse. They hadn't touched since Ava had released Leland's hand outside the club, and now, in the small sterile interior of the lift, the air between them pulsed with some sort of electric current. Ava could feel it deep inside.

CHAPTER FOUR

R ebecca Scott exited the central transit station in Easton and headed toward the Bureau of Security offices. Two men in dark suits parted as she jogged between them up the steps of the sleek, glass-faced structure.

There was no line at the synth unit in the break room as she passed so she paused long enough for a coffee.

Dammit. She burned her tongue on the hot drink as she wound through a cluster of cubicles to get to her desk. Everyone was pretty much gone for the night, so maybe she'd have some peace and quiet to get some work done. There were piles of docs to filter through and there never seemed to be enough hours in the day.

"Are you comfortable?" She rounded the corner to discover Frank, with his feet propped on her desk, talking on his comm unit.

When he saw her, Frank moved so fast he almost toppled backward in his chair. "Beck, I thought you weren't coming back. I was just, uh, making a call to a witness."

Frank had only been with the bureau for two years and still seemed a little intimidated by his more senior partner, Beck. He was twenty-six, slim with clean-cut dark hair and youthful optimism. Beck liked him.

"Tell Sharon I said hello." Sharon and Frank had been dating for about six months and things seemed serious. "And get outta my chair."

He cupped his hand around the mic on his comm unit as he stood up and then he whispered into the phone. "I'll call you later, sweetie. I gotta go."

Rebecca "Beck" Scott used the nickname that her roommate Jenna Bookman had given her in college. Jenna had told her she didn't look like a "Rebecca." Rebeccas were sweet, wholesome, and nothing like the competitive, driven, athletic woman that she was. Rebeccas studied to become elementary school teachers, not investigators for the Federal Bureau of Security. Rebeccas were not trained marksmen. She had the long blond-haired sorority girl looks and a face pretty enough to carry the name, but Rebeccas didn't specialize in hand-to-hand combat, and work for the Bureau, but Beck did.

"If you're going to stick around you can help me read through this latest batch of dispatches." Beck looked up from her chair at Frank. She realized now that he looked tired. "You know what, never mind. You should take Sharon out for dinner. I'll catch up with you tomorrow."

"Are you sure? I can stay if you need me to."

"No, I've got this." Frank had a life; he might as well enjoy it. Beck couldn't remember the last time she'd had a decent dinner date.

"Okay, if you're sure."

"I'm good. Go." As she typed her security code into the terminal, she waved him off. The screen cycled through the machine's encryption field, and as she watched the screen blink she shucked out of her blazer and then rolled her shoulders in slow circles. She reached for the coffee and sipped as she began to scroll through the files she'd been sent.

Beck was tired of making no headway in tracking Meredith. The militant leader of the Return to Earth movement had been infuriatingly elusive since the bombings in Easton. But everyone left a trail of some kind, and Beck was hell-bent on finding Meredith's.

The Return to Earth movement started as a nonviolent group a decade earlier, but in recent months their tactics had taken a decidedly more aggressive turn. Why? What had changed? Was Meredith frustrated that society hadn't bought into her bullshit so she was just going to make her point with bombs? Was it as simple as that?

Beck doubted it. Meredith seemed too smart for that. But maybe she wasn't smart; maybe she was just crazy and the Bureau was giving the movement's leadership too much credit.

Either way, the bombings had shaken Easton and the ruling class to their core. How could a city with such sophisticated surveillance and security not stop such an overt act of terrorism? Beck wondered the same thing. She was missing something, but what?

The whole Return to Earth movement baffled Beck. Why would anyone want to live on the surface? The cities had risen more than a hundred years ago because the Earth had become unfit for humanity. The ground offered nothing but fucked up weather, contaminated water, air quality for shit, and tribes of savage groundlings. Actually, come to think of it, why not just let those who wanted to leave the cloud cities go ahead and leave? The malcontents were always complaining about getting their fair share when really they were all a bunch of pampered whiners. Chancellor Argosy should do society a favor and let the insurgents fend for themselves on the ground.

The main overhead lights dimmed to nighttime power saver level. The computer's display cast an eerie greenish glow on the cubicle wall. She entered a word search. The Argosy name had shown up in encrypted messages the Bureau had intercepted enough times to be considered a credible threat. Beck was looking for leads, connections.

She polished off her coffee as she waited for the search to finish. Beck leaned back in her chair and watched the program run. This might take a while, but that was fine, she had nowhere else to be at the moment.

CHAPTER FIVE

Ava gave Leland a sideways glance as they rode the lift. Leland was staring straight ahead, silently watching the lighted panel chart their climb.

When the lift reached the top floor, Leland motioned for Ava to exit first. She waited as Leland entered a code on the panel near the door. As they stepped in, low lighting flickered on and a soothing female voice greeted them. "Welcome back, Leland."

"Low lights are good, thank you. Flame please." Leland spoke to no one, but the in-room sensors obviously understood, and Ava noticed a simulated fire come to life in front of a sunken sofa in the center of the large open suite. Ava wasn't sure what she'd expected, but this wasn't it. Who was this woman?

Leland rounded a bar near a small kitchen unit and turned toward Ava. "Drink?"

"Please." Ava walked toward the wall of glass overlooking the city. Gazing out over the floating quadrant nearest this vantage point, she could see the edge of Easton. And the deep blackness of nothing just beyond that edge. The horizon swallowed up, invisible, in the darkness of the night. The view of the cityscape was amazing. She would miss Easton, but not enough to stay. She turned away and joined Leland in the kitchen.

Leland held a drink in each hand as she turned to face Ava. With both of Leland's hands occupied, Ava took the opportunity to remove the dark glasses from Leland's face again. Her eyes were dark green. And something in Leland's candid gaze stirred Ava's memory. Her stomach lurched, and she took a step back.

Every citizen in the cloud cities had green eyes. So the color was no surprise. It was a byproduct of eating an exclusively synthetic diet. Ava had only ever met one person who did not have green eyes. Cole. Cole had brown eyes and the same open, vulnerable look that Leland was giving Ava now.

The memory of Cole came rushing back, and along with it, Audrey and Ava's near deadly crash in the mountains. She'd been trying to emotionally distance herself by making a determined effort *not* to think about these things, and now, in an instant, everything came flooding back.

Cole had rescued Ava from a downed aircraft, and after a vicious attack, Ava had taken Cole back to the cloud city of Easton for medical care that didn't exist on the ground. During her recovery, Cole managed to steal her best friend Audrey's heart. She'd felt more than friendship for Audrey but had never acted on it. And then she'd lost her completely.

Audrey left everything for Cole. She was living on the ground where it might as well be the nineteenth century: no power grid, no machines, no technology of any kind. In the end, Ava had had no choice but to deliver Audrey to Cole. After all, Ava loved Audrey. She wanted Audrey to be happy even if that meant finding happiness with someone else.

Ava couldn't understand that sort of sacrifice, the willingness to leave everything for love. Maybe she was selfish. Actually, she knew she was selfish. She couldn't imagine ever making such a decision.

Something about Leland's unguarded gaze brought the memory of the confusion, hurt, and anger she'd felt when she'd found Cole and then lost Audrey. It all rushed back like a flash memory, like a lightning strike.

Leland must have sensed the change in her mood. Leland looked crestfallen. Maybe she expected Ava to dash for the door.

"The bright lights, sometimes they bother my eyes. The glasses also offer a bit of…cover." Leland set the drinks down and leaned back against the raised countertop. "Don't feel any pressure to stay if you'd like to leave—"

"No, it's just that you reminded me of someone." Ava didn't want to explain the entire saga, and she didn't want the memory to ruin their evening. She willed herself to get past it. She shoved the feelings down in her chest and took a step closer to Leland.

Ava took Leland's face in both hands and kissed her. She let her body sink into Leland as they kissed. She no longer wanted the drink. She wanted to feel something. So far everything about Leland had been a surprise. Maybe she'd been dating the wrong type of woman all along.

She released Leland and leaned back a little. She was, after all, in Leland's place. Maybe she should let Leland make the next move.

Leland traced her fingertips down Ava's cheek to her collarbone but didn't let her hand drift further. "You are so beautiful," she whispered. "Are you sure you want to be here?"

Rather than answer, Ava slid the palms of her hands down Leland's chest, under her jacket until her right hand was at Leland's crotch. She began a firm stroke, and Leland stiffened beneath her touch.

Chapter Six

Leland was losing the battle to contain her arousal. Ava's hands slid down Leland's chest, slowly and methodically, pausing as she swept her palms across Leland's breasts, and then Ava's hands drifted across her torso. Her stomach muscles twitched as Ava's fingers lightly connected with skin just below the hem of her untucked shirt. Ava paused there to tease with her fingertips and then let her hand glide down to Leland's crotch. She stroked slowly, and an involuntary groan issued from Leland. She pulled Ava close and kissed her.

Ava began to strip them of their clothes as Leland moved them to the bedroom. They angled for the large bed, littered with pillows.

Ava pushed Leland back onto the bed and straddled her waist. Leland felt suddenly self-conscious and with a word, extinguished the lights. Ambient lumination from nearby buildings still filtered through the open blinds, casting the bedroom in an eerily cool electric glow.

It wasn't that Leland believed she was unattractive. It wasn't that she hadn't been with beautiful women before. But most women sought her company for status, for who they thought she was, for whom they could become if partnered with her. Ava had chosen her for none of those reasons because she had no idea who Leland really was. Ava was here with her, only her.

Separated from her usual façade, she felt oddly exposed. As Ava pressed her nude body against hers, she felt inept. Ava never faltered, seemed so sure of herself as she set upon Leland with her soft, hot mouth.

"Is this okay?" Ava asked as she kissed her way down the center of Leland's chest. She glanced up at Leland, her green eyes piercing Leland's soul even in the low light. "You seem a little distant."

"I'm sorry. I'm just…I think I'm a little in awe of you." Leland drew Ava close so that she could kiss her. "I don't mean to be distant. I'm not distant, really. I'm right here." Why was she having doubts about herself? Every inch of her body was on fire under Ava's touch. She needed to engage fully and let Ava know how she was really feeling about her. Even though they'd just met, she had some otherworldly notion that they shared some deeper connection. That they'd met before, and not just on the tarmac earlier, but in a former life.

She rolled Ava onto her back and slid her leg between Ava's, putting firm contact against the place between Ava's legs. Ava was so wet.

Ava's eyes were closed, and she groaned in response to the rhythmic pressure Leland was applying. When she opened her eyes, she had a look on her face as if she was seeing Leland for the first time.

"I have seen you before. I saw you today on the flight deck."

"Yes." Leland slowed her movements but didn't stop.

"What were you doing there?"

"Picking up some containers of bio material for Easton's lab." Mostly the truth. Leland stopped moving and rested on her elbows, hovering just above Ava's face. "I was regretting that I didn't stop you earlier when I saw you. But then you came to the club." She traced her fingertip along Ava's cheek. "I saw you the minute you walked in. I knew I'd been given a second chance and I didn't want to miss it."

"But then I asked you to dance first."

"Yes, you did."

Leland felt Ava's hands on her ass, pulling her tightly against her. Leland kissed Ava slowly, deeply, as she began to move again. But she sensed that she wasn't giving Ava exactly what she wanted, so she let Ava show her.

Ava shifted beneath her, and Leland let her roll on top again. She took a fistful of Leland's hair and pulled her head back to roughly kiss her neck and shoulders and then her breasts before moving back up to kiss her deeply. Leland wasn't used to being handled roughly, but she decided maybe she liked it. Ava's intensity just served to spike Leland's arousal. Ava grasped Leland's hand and pushed it down between them, between her legs.

"Fuck me." Ava took Leland's ear between her teeth and bit sharply as she said the words. It wasn't a request. It was a command.

Leland was aflame. She stroked with her fingers, but Ava's movements signaled urgency as Ava began to grind against Leland's hand. She slid into Ava slowly at first, but then deeper, with force as Ava rode her hand and arched into each thrust.

Leland was mesmerized as she watched Ava's face above hers. Ava's eyes were closed, and she seemed lost in some erotic thrall, and for a brief instant Leland wondered if Ava were visualizing that she was with someone else. She squelched her insecurities as Ava opened her eyes and gave Leland the most penetrating gaze. Then Ava closed her eyes again and cried out as she leaned back and allowed the orgasm to claim her. Ava threw her head back, and then just as quickly she cried out again and collapsed on top of Leland. Sweat glistened across their skin. They were both breathing hard as Leland kissed Ava's damp forehead.

Ava slid down so that her cheek was against Leland's chest. Her heart thumped like a drum next to Ava's ear. She teased Leland's nipple with her fingers and began to slide slowly down Leland's torso, feathering light kisses as she moved farther down.

She settled between Leland's legs and began to stroke there with her tongue. Leland writhed beneath her, pressing against her mouth.

Ava slipped two fingers inside while she continued to work with her tongue. Leland came hard and fast. She cried out as she climaxed.

As she felt Leland settle, Ava slowly kissed her way back up until she was nestled against Leland's shoulder.

Leland slid the covering that had been cast quickly aside back over them and pulled Ava close.

Ava was trying to relax, but she felt as if every nerve ending in her body was on edge. She shifted restlessly beside Leland, rolling over so that her back was against Leland's chest. She felt Leland's lips brush the back of her neck. Her chest constricted as if she couldn't breathe. An unexpected tear drifted from the corner of her eye and she wiped it away. Why did she feel so strange? She almost felt as if she was having some out-of-body experience. She felt oddly separated from herself.

"Hey, are you okay?" Leland's tone was soft, soothing, not demanding, but still Ava felt defensive.

"I'm fine." She felt her body stiffen involuntarily. *Relax. Just relax.* She tried to bring herself back from the edge. She turned in Leland's arms and gave her a weak smile. She could see by the look on Leland's face that her smile hadn't been very convincing.

"You just seemed, um, I just sensed you were…you seem upset."

She was upset. But why? Was it that flash memory of Cole? Cole, the outlander with brown eyes who'd turned her world upside down. Or was Leland simply a fresh reminder of the thing she didn't have, someone in her life that meant something?

"I should go." Ava moved to the side of the bed. She sat up and ran her fingers through her hair.

"Oh." Leland sounded disappointed.

Well, there wasn't anything Ava could do about it. This was what it was, one night of sex with a stranger. Ava turned to look at Leland. She was on her back with her arm covering her face, her small breasts and slender frame only partially covered by the rumpled sheet. Her flawless olive skin and dark hair contrasted against the white bedding in the light from the windows in such a way that Ava was reminded of some rare, fine painting of a reclined figure on white canvas.

A surge of unexpected emotion washed over Ava like a rogue wave. Regret? Fear? Fear. Panic even. What had just happened between them? She couldn't look away and she didn't move. She was frozen.

After a moment, Leland moved her arm and gave Ava a searching look, but she made no move to touch her. And yet, Ava felt it, as sure as if she had been touched.

"Stay."

Leland's whispered request tugged at Ava as if Leland had reached into her chest with her hand.

She fought her urge to flee, climbed back under the covering, and slid close to Leland. Ava kissed her, slowly, sweetly. She willed herself to relax. She *would* allow herself to feel safe, because something about Leland did make her feel safe.

"Make love to me." Ava spoke against Leland's barely parted lips and then sealed the request with another deep kiss.

Leland rolled on top of her and began to tenderly explore her body. Kissing, stroking, lingering in particularly sensitive places, and with methodical attentiveness, she brought Ava to a powerful reverberating orgasm. And in a rare instance of absolute ecstasy, Ava did something she never allowed herself to do. She relinquished control.

CHAPTER SEVEN

Leland sleepily walked to the kitchen. She leaned on the counter and scanned the suite. The simulated flame from the previous night was still on the hearth in front of the L-shaped white sofa.

"Flame off." Her voice cracked a little, and she reached for water.

She'd slept so soundly she hadn't heard Ava leave. She couldn't remember the last time she'd slept so well. That must be what freedom felt like.

They'd made love until at least three, and still she felt rested. Rejuvenated. Alive. Lately, she'd felt the press of humanity crowding in around her. She was only just beginning her twenty-seventh year, but worry was making her feel seventy. She pressed buttons on the front of the food synthesizer and waited for a protein drink. Then she retrieved a small vial from the other room and measured part of it into the green liquid.

She drank slowly, feeling the texture of the fibrous material she'd just added.

It wasn't like she could save the world. So far her tests were inconclusive at best, which was why she'd started her own human trial, on herself. Maybe she was wrong. She probably was.

Leland closed her eyes and flashed back to her night with Ava. What a gift last night had been. Ava was beautiful and an amazing lover. Forceful, yet tender. Passionate and funny. One night with Ava was the worst sort of tease. But one night was all it was ever going to be. Obviously, Ava hadn't wanted there to be more. She'd left without so much as a good-bye.

Leland sighed and headed toward the shower.

❖

Ava threw two small bags onto the passenger side of her two-seated cruiser. Her apartment was boxed and on a cargo ship, currently somewhere over the central North American continent on its way to CCSF. The last thing to get to the West Coast was herself. She quickly ran through preflight, adjusted her headset, and once she received clearance, she engaged the hydrogen boosters and moved into position in front of the launch tube.

Within minutes, she was winging her way toward land. A ribbon of coastal white sand cut underneath her flight path at right angles, extending south and north as far as she could see. Shortly, she'd be punching through the clouds covering the Blue Mountains. As she traversed the gentle blue ridges, she looked down and thought of Audrey and Cole, which immediately made her think of Leland.

She'd woken in Leland's suite just as the sun was beginning to seep in through the partially closed blinds. Watching Leland sleep soundly beside her, she'd considered waking her up to say good-bye but then decided against it. They were from different cities and apparently had very different lives as was evident from the two guards in dark clothing stationed outside the door as she'd exited the suite. Maybe Leland was some celebrity that Ava had failed to recognize. Or maybe she was the keeper of international secrets. Her life obviously operated at some level where personal security was necessary.

Ava had definitely made the right choice at the club. Actually, she probably had to give Sara all the credit for that. Leland had been a truly unexpected surprise, and Ava's stomach clenched with the sense memory of their night together.

Leland was incredibly sexy. Her slender, elegant body was a sensual delight that Ava could easily have explored for many more hours, but at some point, sleep had claimed them. If Ava hadn't had to report for flight duty in less than twenty-four hours, she might have considered just keeping Leland in bed throughout the next day.

Ava lightly brushed her fingers over her lips and then trailed them down her throat as she remembered the softness of Leland's mouth against hers.

Maybe she should have left a note. When confronted with a situation that potentially involved emotional complications, Ava usually erred on the side of distance and walked away. This might be one time when she'd end up regretting that decision.

CHAPTER EIGHT

Beck checked the readout again and then leaned forward so she could see past the glare on the windshield to read the building number. "Yeah, this is the place. Pull around the corner."

Frank eased out of the morning commute traffic and glided the maglev cruiser into a vacant spot near a refuse station. The vehicle was unmarked, which in Beck's opinion sometimes made it stand out even more.

Beck checked her pulse weapon then slid it back into the holster under her jacket for the short walk back to the address. Frank called in their location.

Beck was first out of the car. Frank fell in behind her as they weaved through people along the pedestrian corridor. Everyone seemed to be in a sleepy haze, heading to work or breakfast or home from an all night club outing perhaps. No one paid them any attention as Beck entered an override code on the keypad next to the nondescript gray steel door. The lock clicked open and Frank followed her inside.

Once in the dark interior, Beck pulled her weapon free. The stair access to the lower levels was just ahead. They descended one flight, two, three, and still no signs of life. She could hear a low rumble and the floor had begun to vibrate slightly from the enormous nuclear powered turbines that kept the cloud city in the air. The engines were still several levels down from their position. They wouldn't reach them because their target was on level five.

It was a different world below street level. Dimly lit and except for the constant hum of the turbines, quiet.

Beck came to a stop and signaled back to Frank that their target was just ahead. He stepped around her with his weapon drawn to position himself on the other side of the door marked VEN6 in large blocky type. She waited for him to nod for her to proceed.

The door wasn't locked. She lowered the handle and then shoved the door open, half expecting to be greeted by a pulse weapon discharge, but there was nothing. Whatever had been happening in this room, they'd missed it.

Beck holstered her gun and kicked at loose paper debris strewn across the floor. Frank picked a few pages up.

"These look like parts of a city schematic."

"That's because that's exactly what they are." She circled behind a rectangular table at the back of the room. All that remained on the table were the coiled remains of remote router connectors and cups of day old coffee.

The insurgents had definitely been using this as a communication hub, but not any longer. *Damn.* Somehow the Return to Earth movement managed to stay one step ahead of the bureau, and it was really starting to piss Beck off.

"Call it in. Get them to send a forensics team." Beck didn't want to touch anything or move anything else until they'd combed the place for breadcrumbs. *Meredith, what's your next move?*

CHAPTER NINE

Leland ran the previous night's specimens through the chromatography machine. Separating the individual components that made the whole would enable her to look for signatures that the microscope wouldn't show. She'd already done a count of microbes under the microscope; now she checked for specific chemical constituents that the GMO had modified to see what the newly introduced bacteria was now affecting. What she saw confirmed her suspicions. The first few silica plates she reviewed had to be rejected for impurities.

The genetically modified plants, components of which were used in various ways to supplement the synthetic manufacture of food, were becoming less and less viable. Urban populations weren't getting the nutrition they needed from the food supply, their immune systems were becoming compromised, and people were getting sick. This newest flu virus was the first warning sign. Likely more would follow.

She pulled a small black notebook from her pocket and made some notes for later review. If anyone had seen her actually make an old school notation on paper they might have considered escorting her from the building, but she wasn't crazy, not even a little. These notations were more secure on paper in her pocket than entered into the system at the lab where they could easily be altered. Oh, yes, she entered the appropriate data in the lab's database, but her personal observations were for her eyes only.

This was the sixth city in three weeks where she'd seen the same strain of microbes exhibited in the samples. The corporate giants of the synthetic nutrition industry were not going to be happy about her findings, if she even got them to listen in the first place. The corporate suits tended to believe that they had control over their scientists and that their scientists could control genes. But genes were messy. And Leland was beginning to believe that science had no real control over such mechanisms.

A pounding sensation behind her eyes signaled the arrival of the headache she'd been trying to keep at bay for over an hour. She tossed the rejected trays into the biohazard bin, stood, and stretched her back.

She pulled an antique watch from her pocket and checked the time. The analog timepiece had been a gift from her maternal grandmother when she'd finished her doctorate. The pocket watch had been delivered with an admonishment to cherish time. Time, the only commodity with any true value, she'd said.

Leland remembered her father's ridicule in response to the gift. The only thing he valued was money.

The watch should probably be at her home, on display, under glass. But Leland had no room in her life for objects that she couldn't use. Besides, every time she felt the watch in her pocket, she thought of her grandmother, who'd been lost to cancer more than a year ago.

She was just about to leave when Jackson came by. He was wearing a mask that covered his mouth and nose.

"Still not feeling well?" Leland asked just to be polite. The truth was Jackson looked like hell. His color was bad, and his red-rimmed eyes looked completely bloodshot. It seemed like a good idea that she'd stepped in and signed for the most recent shipment. He was in no condition to be at work. Leland had been sampling specimens in labs in various cities the past few weeks, and she had yet to uncover patient zero for this virus. She was fairly certain it had originated from an outside source. A carrier perhaps, but whom or what?

"I'm better." He coughed behind the mask.

"Hey, go home and go back to bed. I've already checked all of these samples. There's nothing else that has to be done today."

"Are you sure?" The look in his eyes above the white mask seemed to register relief.

"Yeah, I'm sure. I was just going to take off and see if I could catch a flight out this afternoon."

"How did everything look?" He seemed too tired to stand and slumped onto a nearby stool. His lab coat looked as if he'd slept in it.

"About half of this batch is unusable."

"Really?" He looked at the castoffs in the biohazard bin and shook his head. "This is becoming a trend."

"Yeah." This was beyond trend status, but Leland didn't want to say more. She didn't know Jackson well enough to know where his loyalties lay. "Listen, I'm taking off. Feel better." She hung her lab coat by the door, slid her clearance card through the reader, and exited as the doors slid open.

Her escorts were waiting just outside the containment area. They matched her pace as she headed out to the transport waiting in front of the steel and glass building.

"I'd like to try to catch the last afternoon flight." She spoke to the young driver as he held the door open for her.

"Yes, ma'am." He shut the door and they were en route.

When they reached Easton's flight center, the young man retrieved her single bag from the car. She'd put on a heavier jacket she'd left in the car earlier because the temp had dropped again. She made sure the small notebook was still tucked in the pocket of her slacks. It comforted her to run her fingers over the rounded corners and know that it was still with her. One of her security escorts from the vehicle that had trailed behind them stepped up and took her bag and then ushered her toward the entrance. She knew he would see her safely onto the aircraft. And a security detail would be waiting for her when she touched down. So much for personal space and freedom.

CHAPTER TEN

A va's first day on the job in San Francisco hadn't gone quite as she'd expected. Her assigned copilot, Quinn, wouldn't have been Ava's first pick if given the choice. Lana Quinn was very attractive. Maybe handsome was a better description. She was tall, broad shouldered, leanly muscled, and arrogant. The arrogance wouldn't ordinarily be so annoying to Ava, but there was something else about Quinn that Ava didn't quite trust.

There were many pilots who suffered from supreme confidence bordering on arrogance. That just came with the territory, and Ava had been guilty of it herself from time to time, especially when she first started flying. Back when she thought she was invincible.

Ava powered down the aircraft. They'd just done a quick passenger flight down to CC San Diego. That short route was enough for her to know she was stuck with a copilot she didn't really care for. It was her first day and too soon to ask for a change in assignment without coming off as some high maintenance rookie. She'd have to ride this out for a month or two to have legitimate grounds to ask to be paired with a different pilot.

"Want to get a drink?"

The engines hummed and then were silent, but Ava ignored the question.

"What? Too popular already to grab a drink with me?" Quinn partially unzipped her flight suit as she shifted in her seat. Ava couldn't help but notice cleavage and the edge of some intricate tattoo revealed by the very low-cut T-shirt Quinn was wearing under her flight suit.

"Thanks, but I'm beat. Another time?" Ava logged out of the flight computer and stowed her headset.

"Sure." Quinn stood and partially blocked the cockpit exit.

If Quinn was going to try to use intimidation to wear her down or win her over, it wasn't going to work with Ava. Quinn wasn't going to move so Ava had no choice but to make fleeting physical contact as she slid past and headed across the tarmac. She wanted to get to her new residential cube, shower, and start the slow process of unpacking.

This wasn't the first time Ava had started over in a new city. She'd gone away to CC Houston for flight training. That had lasted for three years. She'd attended college in the cloud city of London before that. London was where Ava had met Audrey. Then they'd both eventually ended up in CC Easton.

Maybe she'd stayed in Easton too long. She'd forgotten what it was like to integrate smoothly into a new living situation. The first step would normally have been to meet friends through work, but Quinn was going to be a huge deterrent for that. Maybe she was just tired. Maybe day two on the job would be better. As she walked toward her new apartment, she hoped the transfer to San Francisco hadn't been a mistake.

Ava decided to walk around a bit before heading to the pile of crates that awaited her at her new apartment. She could see the orange red of the Golden Gate landmark jut up into the airspace between two residential towers and decided to check it out.

A hundred years ago, when the cities had risen and lost connections with features that were significant to their urban identities on the ground, some of them had replicated those structures in the clouds. In San Francisco's case that meant turning one of its primary pedestrian corridors into a replica of the Golden Gate Bridge.

Ava stepped onto the expanse, crowded with people going to and from work, or just crossing from one suspended quadrant to the next. The sun was a giant orange orb behind her, sinking into the Pacific. She stopped midway and leaned over the railing to look east. In the distance, gaps in the fog bank presented glimpses of the rocky Pacific Coast, a breathtaking contrast to the Eastern Seaboard.

The air was cold now. Ava pulled the jacket she wore over her flightsuit more tightly and zipped it up. She blew warm air on her hands as she rubbed them together then shoved them in her pockets. She stood for a few more minutes enjoying the view of the city and the landmass beyond. Shaking off Quinn's disquieting energy, optimism settled again in her chest, and Ava's steps felt lighter as she headed for her new home.

After a few hours arranging her place, Ava decided to take a break and finish the rest of the unpacking another day. She'd done enough to make things functional. Especially since she'd be leaving tomorrow on an overnight international route to CC Amsterdam. She was already dreading a layover with Quinn.

Ava pulled one of her favorite college sweatshirts from an open crate and searched the kitchen for a glass. She poured herself a bourbon and settled onto the sofa with her tablet.

Off and on all day, Leland had crept into her thoughts. She closed her eyes and sank further into the sofa. *Leland James, where are you right now?*

Her tablet pinged. Sara's avatar popped up in the corner of the screen.

"How's it going?"

Ava pulled the tablet into her lap. "Good so far. What are you doing up so late?" If it was nearly nine o'clock on the West Coast, then it was midnight in Easton. She continued to type. "Don't you have to teach eager young minds in the morning?"

"Kelly had to work late, but she'll be here any minute. I just wanted to tell you to have sweet dreams."

"Thanks for thinking of me. Tell Kelly I said hello." Ava clicked off and tossed the tablet onto the sofa.

Tomorrow would be an early day. She might as well turn in, if she could sleep.

CHAPTER ELEVEN

Leland's flight landed around eight thirty, and she was in her apartment by nine. She'd been hopping from city to city so much the past few weeks that her body hardly knew what time zone she was in. She knew she should sleep soon but wasn't sure if she could.

She set her bag down and draped her jacket over a chair. "Dim lights." She spoke to the room sensor. She might not be sleepy just yet, but it had been a long day, and the light in the room was too bright for her tired eyes. The heat kicked on as she moved from the main living space to the bedroom. Hmm, the bed was unmade, just as she'd left it. Tousled sheets reminded her of Ava. Agitated now for sure, she headed back to the computer in the main room.

The icon for new messages blinked at regular intervals. She made herself a protein drink and walked back to the terminal. She tapped in a key code but didn't sit down. She stood at the floor to ceiling window and looked out over the city as several messages played back. The last one was from Richard, her father's personal secretary.

"Leland, I'm calling for your father. He's asked me to confirm that you will attend the dinner with the viceroy from Moscow on the twelfth of this month."

She knew her father was asking for more than her presence at dinner. He'd been making overtures that she should court the viceroy's daughter, whom she'd met and had found incredibly dull. Beautiful, but vacuous. She'd have to find a reasonably weighty reason not to be at that dinner if she had any hope of escaping it. But in the meantime, maybe Richard could help her with a bit of information.

His message continued. "Please contact me tomorrow with your itinerary, and I will relay that information to your father. Formal attire is requested."

Leland sat at the keyboard and began to type. "Richard, message received. I will confirm dinner as soon as I've checked the date against previous engagements on my calendar. Also, I have a request. Can you locate a pilot named Ava Wynne for me? I'll explain later. Thanks, L."

She clicked off and swiveled in her chair. Leland sipped the liquid meal.

She crossed the room and opened a door to stairs leading up. She reached the landing on the second floor and walked through another door into an enclosed greenhouse. The air in the room felt thick with moisture as she moved down the narrow aisle between rows of plants. Every so many feet, Leland stopped, looked closely at a leaf or flower, checked drip lines, and sifted the vermiculite between her fingertips. At the back of the room, she checked the temperature and adjusted it slightly up.

The plants required manual pollination, and since Leland had been traveling so much of late, her maintenance of this task had fallen behind. The task involved the transfer of pollen with an artist's brush or cotton swab, moving pollen from the male flower to the female. Sometimes she removed the corolla from male flowers and brushed the flower itself against the stigmas of female flowers.

Leland found the task oddly erotic. And in this instance, it reminded her of the night she'd spent with Ava. She let out a long sigh and sank back onto a nearby stool. Working with her plants in this small sanctuary of green usually soothed her soul. Tonight it only made her lonely.

After a bit more greenhouse maintenance, she closed the door and headed back downstairs.

She kicked off her shoes and moved to the bedroom. The pocket watch felt smooth between her fingers. It wobbled just a little as its rounded back settled for the night on the bedside table. As usual, the watch was a reminder of her grandmother, whom Leland missed greatly. She missed her mother also, but her mother had been more aligned with her father in terms of his vision for Leland's life. Her grandmother had been her only advocate on the occasions when she'd made attempts to defend her choices to her parents. She'd chosen biochemistry over finance, but having shadowed her father in her early twenties, she was well versed in politics. Despite their sometimes philosophical differences, her father had been open with her about the finances of the world economy and what it took to lead. Despite his attempts to mentor Leland to assume his position, the older she got the further apart she and her father seemed to grow in both interests and ideology. They would reach an impasse sooner than she liked. She wouldn't be able to dodge succession forever. The last time she'd seen him it seemed as if he'd aged ten years in six months. Leland suspected that his health was waning, but neither he nor Richard, nor his current consort would confirm her suspicions. He was probably suffering from the same deficiencies as everyone else, but at his age, he was even more vulnerable.

She reached for the tablet on the other bedside table and clicked through her calendar. The twelfth for dinner was doable. Maybe she should try to make an appearance, despite the viceroy's daughter. She needed to talk with her father about her findings and his plan for succession. Putting it off wasn't going to make the conversation any easier.

CHAPTER TWELVE

The flight to Amsterdam was a long one, but not the longest route Ava had flown. This particular aircraft carried both passengers and cargo to the Dutch cloud city. Four hours into the flight, Quinn had taken a break for food and the lavatory. As she settled back into the pilot's chair to Ava's left, Quinn nodded in her direction. Ava gave her a quick nod back. It was her turn to leave the cockpit.

She walked down the far right aisle through the passenger compartment. Darkness pressed against the windows as they flew toward the sunrise yet to appear. The cabin lights were dim, and most of the passengers dozed under blankets. Ava reached the back and stepped through the curtain into the crew galley area. The space was small. Immediately, a young woman jumped from her seat. She had short blond hair and a petite figure. She was girlish in manner and cute, kid sister cute.

"Can I get you something?"

"Yes, could I get a coffee, um…" Ava was struggling to remember the woman's name.

"Leslie."

"Yes, of course, sorry, Leslie."

"And that's Christopher." Leslie pointed in his direction.

Ava nodded to the man who'd been in the seat next to Leslie when she'd first entered the galley. "Christopher. Right. Sorry."

"Not to worry. This is your first day with the CCSF flight crew, right?"

Ava nodded.

"I have a hard time remembering names too when I meet a group of people all at once." Leslie reached for a carafe of coffee and poured it. "Cream? Sugar?"

"Just a little cream, thanks."

"I'll go do a walk-through and see if anyone needs anything." Christopher left them alone in the galley.

Ava accepted the coffee from Leslie and leaned against the wall. She peered through the small window in the emergency exit door. Moonlight bounced and scattered across the dark ocean surface beneath them as she sipped the hot drink. She turned back when she realized Leslie was watching her.

"How long have you lived in CCSF?" Ava wasn't really in the mood for small talk, but Leslie had been friendly so Ava decided to be friendly back.

"About three years now. It's a great city. You'll love living there."

Ava hoped Leslie was right about that. "Does the entire crew usually stay in the same hotel in Amsterdam?" They'd be in the city for one night before making the return trip.

"Usually. Have you been to Amsterdam before?"

"Yes, but it's been a while. It's a beautiful city."

"I think Quinn and Christopher are planning to go to De Wallen after they drop their bags at the hotel."

Of course the first thing Quinn would do was hit Amsterdam's red light district. Good, then at least she wouldn't have to worry about avoiding Quinn after they arrived. De Wallen was the last place Ava wanted to be tonight, and especially not with Quinn. The sensation of Leland was still with her. She wasn't anxious just yet to have sex with another woman and overwrite that memory.

She realized Leslie was waiting for a response. "I'll probably just get dinner, maybe take a walk along the canal." The elite in CC Amsterdam had managed to create a shallow canal that circled the museum district in the central city, a nostalgic remnant of their urban identity on the ground.

"Would you mind company?"

Leslie's question caught Ava off guard, and she couldn't think quickly enough of an excuse to say no. "Sure, that would be nice." She gave Leslie a weak smile. She hoped Leslie didn't think this would be a date.

"It's hard to be away from my boyfriend so soon. We only just started seeing each other a month ago, and the overnight flights are the worst."

Ava's shoulders relaxed. Not a date. "I've found that the travel can be hard on relationships, but not impossible. As long as both people are fairly independent." She thought briefly of Jenna Bookman and her wife, Sophie. They accommodated Jenna's travel schedule by having an open relationship. That was one way to deal with separation. That approach wasn't for Ava. If she ever did fall in love, she wouldn't be the sort who'd want to share. She'd rather be single. Much simpler. Life was much less stressful without the obligations a relationship would bring.

"Luckily, I'm mostly on West Coast routes." Leslie's voice brought Ava's attention back to the present.

"Well, shall we meet in the lobby and then find a spot to eat?" Ava finished her coffee and looked around for a logical place to stow it. She wasn't sure where to put used dishware since this galley seemed to be set up differently from what she was used to.

"Here, I'll take that." Leslie took the cup from her hand. "Dinner sounds good. I'll just change after we check in and then meet you in the lobby."

Ava nodded and headed back toward the cockpit.

"Leslie is cute isn't she?" Quinn spoke just as she got her headset settled.

How did she always seem to annoy Ava so quickly? Ava hated the feeling that Quinn was paying any attention to what she was doing or whom she was talking with. It was probably just a guess since there were only two other crewmembers on this flight with them, but still, it was annoying.

"Yes, she is." Ava checked airspeed and altitude.

"Do you think she'd be up for night maneuvers after landing?" Quinn smirked.

Seriously? Ava was sure Quinn could see the disgusted expression on her face. Ava shook her head and didn't respond.

"What?"

"Don't talk to me, okay?" Ava felt like she'd need a shower just from the proximity of her seat to Quinn's.

"Whatever. You know, we could run this town if you weren't so uptight."

"You're still talking." Ava knew she probably sounded like an asshole. She didn't care. They had to work together for now, but the minute they stepped out of the aircraft, she wanted to be as far away from Quinn as possible.

The rest of their flight was without incident and without conversation. Quinn finally got the hint.

The lights of the cloud city of Amsterdam glinted in the distance when Ava pulled the microphone attached to her headset close to her lips. "We are making our final approach to the landing platform in CCA. The temperature in Amsterdam is a brisk forty degrees." She clicked off the mic for a second before continuing. "From the flight deck, let me be the first to welcome you to CCA. I hope you've enjoyed your flight. We'll be landing shortly. Flight crew, prepare the cabin."

After touchdown, Quinn left her chair first. Ava was glad. She wanted to give Quinn a head start. She lingered for a minute to log some data into the onboard computer, then Ava made her way back through the cabin to the rear exit. It was her habit to make one pass through the aisles at the end of a flight just to make sure everything was prepped for the cleaning crew. As she stepped into the galley, she realized Quinn was still on board. She had Leslie wedged against the wall, saying something that Ava couldn't quite make out.

Quinn wasn't actually touching Leslie, but she had an arm on either side of her, palms against the wall. She towered over Leslie's petite frame.

"You okay, Leslie?" Ava asked.

When Quinn dropped one arm to turn and look at Ava, Leslie quickly escaped. "I'm good, thanks. I'll see you at the hotel."

"I'll walk with you." Ava stepped past Quinn and ushered Leslie down the steps toward a waiting crew transport. They climbed aboard and Quinn leaned against the doorframe of the rear exit and watched as the transport pulled away.

"Thank you." Leslie touched Ava's arm.

"For what?"

"Quinn."

"Don't worry about it."

"She's a bit of a bully isn't she?"

"She's something all right." Ava didn't want to say more, but she could have.

It was a ten-minute ride to the hotel to check in and freshen up. Ava was waiting in the lobby for Leslie when Quinn and Christopher walked up. They were obviously on their way out for the evening.

"Go ahead, Chris. I'll catch up with you." Quinn stopped next to Ava and motioned for Christopher to continue. He nodded and trotted down the front steps of the hotel.

Ava waited for Quinn to say something. Her guard was already up, in defense mode.

"Listen, Ava. I wanted to apologize."

Well, that was the last thing she expected from Quinn.

"I think we got off on the wrong foot, and I'm sure it's my fault. I speak before I think. I like to play the field, and I think I just made assumptions that you were the same way. Can we just start over?" Quinn extended her hand to Ava.

What choice did she have but to accept the apology? Maybe Quinn was right. Maybe they just made assumptions about each other and the misunderstanding escalated. She accepted Quinn's offered hand.

"Good. I'm glad I caught up with you so we could clear the air." A grin slowly spread across Quinn's face as she released Ava's hand. "Oh, I get it now."

Ava turned to see what Quinn was smiling about. Leslie was approaching them across the lobby. "It's not what you think."

"Sure." Quinn turned to follow in Christopher's footsteps. "Have a nice evening, ladies."

"Did I interrupt something?" Leslie asked.

"No, just an apology that should have been for you. Come on, let's go get some food."

They turned left out of the hotel to walk along the canal. Perfectly shaped artificial ornamental trees were placed at regular intervals along the pedestrian walk that bordered the shallow channel. Each sculpted tree was entwined with tiny white lights. The reflected points of light danced on the wind-rippled surface of the water from the trees and from the windows of nearby buildings. The combined effect of all these details was magical, and Ava wished for a moment that Leland was with her, walking arm in arm. The romantic musing surprised her. Ava never thought of herself as the romantic type.

It had been a while since Ava had walked the streets of CCA, but if memory served there was a good restaurant just ahead.

Leslie's comm unit pinged. "Oh, I'd like to get this if you don't mind. It's my boyfriend."

"Go ahead." As luck would have it, they were only a few yards from the Van Gogh museum, and it looked as if it was still open. "I'll take a look in there. Just come find me when you're ready. No rush." Ava pointed toward the museum as she left Leslie by the canal. Leslie nodded and settled onto a bench.

The museum was closing in a half hour. Hardly any patrons remained in the spacious, modern great hall. Ava breezed through the first two small galleries just off the main room. She was looking for her favorite piece of Van Gogh's work.

The tranquility of the museum soothed Ava. Memories of field trips with her college art history class came back to her as she strolled past the paintings pitched and reeled in blazes of yellow. A sunburst over writhing corn caught her eye, and she paused her tour to soak it in. Art history had been a curious diversion from her core curriculum. Most of it she didn't understand, but this work, Van Gogh's work, somehow spoke to her on a visceral level.

His canvases were dense with visible brushstrokes rendered in a bright, opulent palette. These paintings seemed to provide a direct sense of how the artist viewed each scene, interpreted through his eyes, mind, and heart. His idiosyncratic, emotionally suggestive style affected Ava for some reason. As she stood in front of her favorite piece, *Starry Night*, she felt her own interior, emotional life reflected in the scene. This was a swirling, tumultuous depiction of the night sky. In Ava's opinion, this was a painting beyond the representation of the physical world. This painting was about something else entirely.

"Evocative, is it not?"

Ava hadn't noticed the woman standing near her until she spoke. She was unusually tall, with a mane of long, wavy silver hair and a hooded gray coat that hung past her knees. She turned to look at Ava. In Ava's momentary unguarded emotional state, the woman's fierce gaze was unsettling.

"Hey, there you are." Leslie appeared out of nowhere. "Sorry that took so long. I'm ready if you are."

When Ava looked back, the woman was gone, and for a second Ava wondered if she'd ever even been there in the first place.

Ava nodded. "Yeah, I'm ready."

Leslie hooked her arm through Ava's as they aimed for the exit.

They were lucky to get a table. The restaurant Ava had remembered was obviously still very popular. But they only had to wait for a few minutes before they were seated.

As she studied the menu, Ava noticed a cluster of men and women in dark suits near the entrance. An elderly man appeared in their midst. Then the entire group moved toward a booth near the back of the restaurant. Ava recognized the elderly gentleman right away. Chancellor Argosy was striking. His tanned, olive complexion was crowned by silver hair. He carried himself as if he was royalty, and in fact, he was the monarch of the ruling elite.

When the cities had risen to the clouds a century ago, they had formed a world government in which each city was lead by a viceroy who reported to the head of the central governing body, the chancellor. And thus, neo-feudalism was born. Initially, city citizens had accepted this system as necessary to protect a certain way of life, basically a standard of living well beyond those who were left on the ground to live or die based on their own rugged individualism. However, even in the urban cloud cities, through the years, the widening of the wealth gap had continued, and corporations were given far too much power by the ruling elite.

Ava didn't consider herself particularly political, but she did have some strong feelings about the ruling elite. She'd even fallen out with her mother over what she believed were her mother's prejudices against anyone who didn't run in her same economic class. She and her mother had had a huge confrontation when Ava had brought Cole back to Easton. She was embarrassed by her mother's views and her complete dismissal of Cole as lesser in some way. She hadn't spoken to her mother in months.

Amsterdam was considered the financial capital of the world so it was no huge surprise to see Argosy here. Ava had to laugh that she'd chosen the same place to dine as the leader of the elite ruling class.

She returned to her menu, and after they ordered, she decided to find out a bit more about Leslie. They weren't on a date, but Ava liked Leslie. Maybe they'd become friends.

"So, how did you and your boyfriend meet?" Ava sipped synthetic red wine and sank back into her chair.

"Well, it's sort of a funny story. My girlfriend dumped me for some art student from Paris and Ben's was the shoulder I cried on. He and I had mutual friends. One thing led to another, and well, we started dating."

That explained the lesbian vibe Ava had been getting from Leslie. She knew her sensors weren't that far off. The instances of subtle physical interaction and eye contact had been enough for Ava to question Leslie's gender preference.

"Has it been hard to switch from dating a woman to dating a man?" Ava was genuinely curious.

"It's different, but there are things I'm enjoying about men that I never thought I would."

That made Ava smile. Her mind went to the biggest difference, additional equipment that some women found enjoyable.

As if reading her mind, Leslie blushed. "And I don't mean just that."

"Sorry, I'm not making fun. It's just that, well, my mind automatically went there."

"What about you? Are you seeing anyone?" asked Leslie.

"Not seriously, or at all really—" Movement near the front of the restaurant pulled Ava's attention away from their conversation. People seated nearest the door seemed to be scrambling away from their tables, and then Ava saw him, a man with a gun. He held the pulse weapon out in front with both hands, aimed in the chancellor's direction just behind where Ava and Leslie were seated.

Leslie had her back to the door and couldn't see what was happening. Ava lunged for her and knocked Leslie to the ground just as the pulse weapon reverberated across their table. Wine glasses and dishware shattered in the wake of the pulse discharge.

Chaos erupted from the chancellor's table as a flurry of dark suits were set in motion. The gunman shouted, "Return to Earth," and then fired a second shot.

The blast from another weapon sounded from near the back of the restaurant, and Ava saw the insurgent tossed backward from the force of the shot, a direct hit to his chest. His body convulsed and then was still.

Ava raised up just enough to see that the assassin had missed his mark. The chancellor appeared to be shaken up a bit, but not harmed. But one of his security personnel was on the ground, not moving.

"Are you okay?" Ava moved off Leslie. She'd been partially covering her with her body.

"I'm fine, but you're hurt." Leslie sounded alarmed.

"No, it's just red wine." Ava inspected her ruined shirt, splattered with spots of dark red from her shattered wine glass. She opened and closed her fingers into a fist in an attempt to get her hands to stop trembling.

Sirens sounded outside the restaurant, and within minutes, the place had been quarantined as Chancellor Argosy's security detail interviewed everyone at the scene.

After what seemed like forever, Ava and Leslie were released to return to their hotel, dinner forgotten and hunger beaten back by nerves so that all Ava wanted when she reached the hotel was a drink. She stopped in the bar before heading up to her room.

Alone with her thoughts, she sipped the brown liquor in her glass slowly, letting its warmth ease down her throat. It wasn't as if she liked Argosy, or agreed with his politics, or his greed for that matter, but she also didn't support killing someone just because you didn't like them. The entire event had shaken Ava up.

Her friend Sara had tried to pull Ava into involvement with the Return to Earth movement. She'd initially considered the insurgents to be malcontents and pseudo-socialists. But after spending time with Cole on the ground, Ava wondered if there wasn't some merit to the movement's basic argument. Maybe leaving the ground for the clouds had stripped away some intrinsic element of their existence that gave life meaning. Maybe man was never meant to live so separated from nature.

It didn't really matter, because the ruling elite would never give up their standard of living to return to life on the ground. And Ava wasn't sure she wanted to live on the ground either. She liked her life. Being a pilot was what she loved, and she could only do that as a cloud city resident.

Ava rubbed her temple with her fingers. Her head was throbbing, and the alcohol wasn't dulling the ache. She probably needed to eat something. She waved the bartender over. She'd get some food, take it to her room, and hope for a good night's sleep.

CHAPTER THIRTEEN

B eck was heading back to the bureau after her regular three o'clock coffee shop break when her comm unit buzzed in her pocket. She sipped her drink as she glanced at the screen. A surge of anger raced through her system as she read the text marked urgent. *Fuck.* She dialed Frank.

"I'm getting on the next flight to Amsterdam." She'd changed direction and was walking back toward her apartment.

"Do you want me to go with you?"

"No, stay here. Keep an eye on the chatter. Send me anything that even remotely seems like a lead. I'll share what you find with the team when I get there." Beck clicked off and cut across the street at a fast clip.

Beck had been transferred from the chancellor's personal security detail six months earlier to join the terrorist task force in Easton. But the chancellor's safety was still of personal interest to her so this attempt on his life hit a little too close to home. She didn't know what assistance she could offer the team on the ground in Amsterdam, but she needed to be there. And hopefully she'd have the opportunity to interview the shooter.

As she folded a few shirts and stowed them in a small suitcase she looked around and thought, not for the first time, that her residential unit had all the warmth of a hospital ward. She'd been here six months and still hadn't decorated the walls or bought any furnishings beyond the minimum. Basically, she worked all the time. Her job was her life. But even still, this was a sad excuse for a home.

If she met women out at clubs she never brought them to her place; she usually followed them to theirs. But she needed to get serious about creating a life for herself, a real life, not just a work life.

Yeah, she'd work on that when she returned from Amsterdam. After all, she wasn't getting any younger.

Note to self, get a life.

Beck shouldered the small carryon bag. "Lights off."

The room lights dimmed as she exited.

❖

The forensics team had cleared the site of the shooting by the time she arrived in Amsterdam, but the shooter had not yet been transferred to the incarceration unit. Beck was in luck. IU467 was the prisoner's next stop, but there'd been a delay getting a medical transport so he was still under guard in the hospital in Amsterdam when Beck arrived.

She flashed her badge to the officer stationed at the shooter's door. She'd call him a suspect except the entire event had been captured on security cameras inside the restaurant. He'd definitely shot at the chancellor. The only unknown was why.

He looked in her direction as she entered the room. He looked to be in his mid thirties with one arm cuffed to the metal rail of the bed and bandages all across his chest and shoulder. He turned his head when she closed the door.

"I'm Rebecca Scott with the Bureau of Security. I'd like to ask you a few questions before your transfer to the IU." She pulled a chair next to the bed. His eyes were puffy and he had a drowsy look about him, but otherwise he seemed lucid.

Argosy's security detail had wounded him when they returned fire, once in the chest, once in his shoulder. He'd live. She wondered if he was happy about it.

"Your name is William Michaelson?" She'd read the initial incident report, so she knew his name, but she wanted him to confirm it.

"Will."

"Excuse me?"

"I go by Will, not William."

"Got it." Beck flipped through a small tablet she'd pulled from her bag. "I have a few questions for you."

"I don't have more to say about what happened."

"I just have a couple of follow-up questions if you don't mind. Were you acting on orders from Meredith when you fired on Mr. Argosy?"

"I don't know who the message came from. I already told the other officers that."

"So you get an anonymous message and you just agree to go shoot Mr. Argosy? That seems like a big leap."

Will didn't respond. Okay, she'd try a different tactic.

"Did someone in the Return to Earth movement offer you transport to the ground if you agreed to shoot Mr. Argosy?"

"The elite make us afraid of what's on the ground so that we'll stay in the cities."

"That doesn't really answer my question. But let me just add that the ground is unhealthy, quarantined a century ago for your protection."

"Elitist propaganda."

"Yeah, I've heard the speeches." Beck's idealistic girlfriend in college dragged her to more than one meeting when the movement was in its infancy and was just beginning to infiltrate college campuses. Back when the Return to Earth movement was just an idea. The problem with ideas, even bad ones, is that they're social. They spread like germs through susceptible populations.

"Argosy and the others don't want us to leave the cities. Who would be left to clean the streets or take out the trash?" Will coughed, and Beck offered him a cup of water from a tray table nearby. He took a few sips through a straw.

"So you shot at the chancellor because you're what, a janitor?"

"I'm a teacher."

"Is that why your aim was so far off? How did you get a pulse weapon anyway?" Beck already knew that Will was a teacher, but she was trying to bait him so he'd talk.

He turned and looked directly at her, but didn't speak. His gaze was a bit unnerving. There was a serenity about Will that Beck hadn't expected. He didn't seem like a member of some lunatic fringe; he seemed sane.

"You'd like to leave the city?" Beck pushed him for more.

"Yes, but how would any of us reach the surface unless we brought the whole platform down?" That was the assumed theory behind the earlier bombing that had almost caused Easton's total collapse.

"And then what? You'd swim to shore?" The cloud city of Easton, like all the other cloud cities, hovered over the open sea. They needed access to seawater for basic infrastructure systems: cooling the turbines and desalinization to name two.

"Officer Scott, you seem like a smart woman. You must realize that the ruling elites ensure that the established leadership is subservient to an ideology. In this case, the separation from the ground and the empty worship of commerce."

Beck leaned back in her chair to prepare herself for the whole sales pitch. She hadn't heard it since college and she wondered if the pitch had changed. So far, not much.

"Society has permitted our oligarchs to orchestrate the largest income inequality gap in the history of the world." Will paused and took another sip of water. "The ruling elite have convinced us to abandon the majority of the Earth's population on the ground—never to benefit from the wealth that we, the few, the city dwellers, benefit from on a daily basis up in the clouds. But to what end? We have forsaken our ancestors. We have forsaken our earthly birthright. We have abandoned the real for the synthetic."

"I think life is pretty good here. Everyone has healthcare, no one goes hungry, everyone has work—"

"Many have work without meaning. That's not the same thing as freedom."

Beck was silent. Will was obviously well versed in the movement's ideology. And that was how far the movement had come...from the spark of an idea to an ideology.

Once again, she wondered why the chancellor didn't just give this dissatisfied minority what they wanted, a one-way ticket to the ground. But then maybe Will had a point about who would clean the streets and take out the garbage.

That was what happened when individuals came together to form a society. Not everything could be equal. Beck believed in the end everyone benefited from the shared system. But then again, she enjoyed her work. She was lucky.

"I didn't kill him did I?" Will's tone was even and held no emotion that Beck could sense.

"No. The chancellor was unharmed." Beck stood up. She could tell she wasn't going to get any info of value from Will.

"It doesn't matter." He muttered as if he was talking to himself.

"What did you say?" She turned back.

"It doesn't matter that he wasn't hit. The diversion was what mattered."

"Diversion?"

"I'm tired now." He smiled at Beck. "Good luck with your investigation, Officer."

CHAPTER FOURTEEN

When Ava read the flight docket two days later in CCSF, frustration spread through her entire system. "What's this?" She held the tablet out for Quinn to see.

"It's a babysitting job." Quinn zipped up her flight suit and riffled through her gear bag. They were standing outside the crew lounge. Several pilots passed them on their way to the flight deck.

"Now we're supposed to be a glorified air taxi for some rich kid?"

"That looks to be the size of things." Quinn didn't seem to care one way or the other.

"Why doesn't this bother you?"

"Look, we get to fly either way, and I love to fly. Why does it matter how many passengers we have?"

"It just seems like such a misuse of resources, not to mention our time, to fly one person across the country. And then we're just supposed to hang around and wait to take the chancellor's kid to the next location? Why can't this...Miss Argosy, take a commercial flight?"

"I suppose because of security issues."

The episode with the gunman in CC Amsterdam came rushing back, and Ava felt a knot of nerves in her gut. Maybe the kid would have flown commercial, but probably not now. Great.

"Coming?" Quinn began walking toward the hangar with her gear bag over her shoulder.

"I'll be there. I just need a few." Ava took several minutes in the lounge to try to temper her annoyance. Why did she care? It wasn't like the royal family was wasting her money, just her time. Which she valued highly.

As she neared the aircraft, Ava could see a small security detail flanked someone who was too tall to be a kid. The entire group had their backs toward Ava. She moved past them to climb the stairs when a familiar face cut into her peripheral vision. Leland.

What the hell was Leland doing here with the security detail? As soon as Ava formulated the question in her mind, the pieces of the puzzle began to click into place. She tried to mask the shock she felt as she stepped past Leland and climbed the stairs into the aircraft. Her heart rate spiked as she looked back to confirm what she'd seen.

Quinn remained on the tarmac speaking with the two security guards. Ava left her to deal with the details as she settled into the pilot's chair. What the hell?

Ava entered her personal avionic security code to gain access to the aircraft's onboard computer and was moving through the preflight checklist when Quinn joined her.

"You didn't want to meet her highness before takeoff?" Quinn's tone was mocking.

"No."

"What's wrong?" Quinn asked.

"I'm fine. Just…nothing." Ava busied herself with the flight plan in the onboard computer. She could hear Leland behind her saying something to the departing security team, then the sounds of the ground crew closing the exit door.

"The security team doesn't travel with her?" Ava asked. She figured this might be part of the briefing Quinn had gotten on the tarmac while she made tracks for the safety of the cockpit. She had a million questions, most of which only Leland could answer.

"It seems they do not travel with her if she doesn't want them to. Since she's the only one on the flight, she must think she doesn't need them." Quinn didn't look up from her tasks at the controls as she spoke. "Another security detail will meet us when we touch down in CC Miami. We're to stay onboard with the door sealed until they arrive."

Ava tried to settle. She was having a hard time interpreting her emotions. Was she angry, happy, excited, or all of those feelings at the same time? She was still trying to sort things out as they hovered and rotated out of the hangar bay and shot out of the launch tube heading east toward the cloud city of Miami. CCM would be a four-hour flight, plenty of time to get a few answers from Leland.

"By the way, our passenger is not a kid."

"I noticed." Ava was trying to distract herself with the tasks required to fly the aircraft, with limited success.

"She's sexy as hell. Did you get a good look at her?" Quinn looked over at Ava with a sly grin on her face.

Not again. Okay, the next emotion that erupted to the surface was definitely anger. "Don't say that."

"What? I know Leslie's off limits, but now I'm not allowed to even comment on her royal highness of tall, dark, and gorgeousness?"

Ava shot Quinn a look that she hoped said *shut up*. "I'm getting a coffee."

"Already? We've only been in the air fifteen minutes."

"Do you want one or not?" Ava stood and waited for Quinn to place a drink order.

"No, thanks. I'm good."

Ava walked into the spacious passenger compartment, empty save for one seat. Leland looked up as she stopped in the aisle beside her.

"Hi." Leland's expression seemed tentative.

Ava shook her head and pointed toward the galley. She didn't want Quinn hearing any of what she was about to say to Leland. And for the first minute, Ava couldn't even speak, she paced back and forth across the small space, occasionally glancing at Leland.

"I'm—"

Ava held up her hand to cut Leland off. The pacing continued. After another minute, she finally stopped in front of Leland, hands on her hips.

"What the hell is going on?"

"I requested you for this flight. I wanted to see you." Leland seemed a bit sheepish. "I had hoped you'd want to see me."

"Who are you?"

Leland sighed. "Leland James...Argosy."

"Argosy? Argosy!"

"I'm sorry I didn't tell you, but—"

"I can't fucking believe this." Ava had slept with the chancellor's daughter. Her father had more accumulated wealth than anyone in the free world. "I can't believe you lied to me."

"I was afraid if you'd known who I really was, you wouldn't have wanted to be with me."

"Well, now we'll never know will we?" Maybe she would and maybe she wouldn't have. She wasn't sure. But now the security detail at the hotel and the driver, and the penthouse suite, it all made sense. Ava was stupid for not figuring out something wasn't adding up from the very beginning. She was so taken with Leland that she hadn't wanted to examine things too closely.

"You shouldn't be traveling alone." Now realizing who Leland was and having just recently witnessed the shooting in Amsterdam, she was worried that Leland was being too cavalier. "Why did you let your security detail stay behind? And the flight docket said you also declined additional service crew. Why?"

"I wanted some privacy on this flight to talk with you. You don't understand what it's like to never have the opportunity to move freely, without oversight."

"No, I don't." Regardless of having never experienced that kind of life on display, Ava knew she wouldn't like it.

"I shouldn't have asked for you for this flight. I'm sorry." Leland seemed genuinely crestfallen. "I just assumed...well, I assumed that you enjoyed that night we spent together in Easton as much as I did. I should have realized that wasn't the case when you didn't leave your number or say good-bye. I sincerely apologize."

Leland turned to go back to her seat, but Ava stopped her with her hand on her arm. "Leland, wait. I'm the one who's sorry."

Leland partially turned back toward her.

"Listen, I did enjoy our night together." She'd more than enjoyed it. She hadn't been able to stop thinking about it. Ava stepped closer. "I regretted not leaving you a note or something. I was just—" Ava shifted her gaze and looked toward the front of the aircraft.

"What?"

"Did you feel that?" Ava realized she still had her hand on Leland's arm and dropped it to her side.

"Feel what?"

"We just changed direction." Ava started to take a few steps toward the cockpit but turned back. "Just wait here for a minute. I'll be right back."

When she got to the cockpit, she was even more confused. Quinn's seat was empty. She glanced at navigation but didn't take her seat. The autopilot had been engaged. They had definitely deviated from the flight path. The aircraft was headed southeast and had begun a slow descent.

Ava was about to go back to the galley for Leland when she heard muffled voices behind her. She stopped dead in her tracks as she stepped back into the passenger compartment. Quinn had Leland pressed into a seat in the front row of the compartment and was holding a handheld pulse weapon against her temple.

"Quinn, what the fuck is going on?" Ava's mind raced. Could she get back to the cockpit fast enough to retrieve the sidearm in the compartment near her seat?

"Don't bother." Quinn waved the other gun in her free hand as if reading her mind. "We're going to take a little trip to the desert. And everyone is just going to relax."

"Quinn, give me the gun." Ava took a step forward.

"Here's what's going to happen. You're going to go back to your chair and you're going to follow the new navigation coordinates, and you're going to land this bird where I say you're going to land it." Quinn motioned for Ava to go back to the cockpit.

"No, I'm not. I don't know what's going on here, but I'm not letting you hijack this aircraft. Not on my watch."

"Is that so?" A smile spread slowly across Quinn's face, then abruptly turned into a sneer. She struck Leland across the face with the hand she was still gripping the weapon with. Blood was at the corner of Leland's mouth. Ava took a step forward, and Quinn struck Leland again.

"Okay, okay! Stop!" Ava held her hands in front of her, palms out, hopefully to signal surrender.

Quinn hit Leland again, twice, in rapid succession, almost in a wrathful frenzy, as if she was working out some other demon that had nothing to do with the situation at hand.

"Quinn! Fucking stop!" Ava moved toward Quinn again. Quinn swiveled and aimed the pulse weapon in Ava's direction.

"You think you're some kind of hero don't you? A regular Captain America, here to save the day." Ava could see that Leland was in pain. She was bleeding from her nose and her lip. "Well, Cap, this is one ship you can't save. Now get your ass in the chair and land this bird."

"Okay, I'm going. Please don't hit her again."

Quinn dropped into a chair across the aisle from Leland as Ava moved back to the cockpit.

Fuck. Fuck. Fuck. She should have listened to her gut about Quinn. She'd had a weird feeling about her from the first day they'd flown together. That apology in Amsterdam had just been a smokescreen. *Think, Ava, think.*

She adjusted her headset. The cockpit door was open so Quinn could easily see what she was doing from where she was seated. For a moment, she debated the best way to signal their situation to avionic control. As if anticipating Ava's next move, Quinn shouted from her seat in the front row of the passenger compartment.

"And I've disabled the black box, so just fly the damn aircraft. By the time flight control figures out we're off course we'll be on the ground and off the grid."

Ava's cheeks flamed hot. How could they end up somewhere off the grid? There was no such thing. The grid was everywhere. What the hell was Quinn talking about? Anger constricted her chest. She hated to give Quinn even the smallest ounce of control over the situation, but with Leland at gunpoint, there was nothing else she could do. If Quinn fired the pulse weapon, Leland would be dead and she'd be next. Not to mention the danger of detonating a pulse round on board. The aircraft would decompress and then they'd all be screwed. Getting the plane on the ground was the safest route. Then she could trigger the emergency beacon and hope someone would come get them. Leland definitely picked the wrong flight to leave her security detail behind. She'd probably trusted that Ava and her copilot weren't psychotic. Well, she'd been half right.

CHAPTER FIFTEEN

Leland's lip throbbed. She pulled her shaking hand away from her face to see that her fingertips had blood on them. Quinn shifted between watching Ava in the cockpit to watching her. Leland focused on making herself as small as possible in the seat across the aisle from Quinn. She didn't fancy any further contact with Quinn's fist. The woman seemed a bit unstable. And angry, very angry.

After the attack on her father in CC Amsterdam, he'd cautioned her not to travel without security. Why hadn't she listened to him? She'd dismissed him as being overprotective. Now she was good and rightly screwed and Ava along with her. Damn.

The idea that she could be a normal citizen, that she could lead a normal life, was pure fiction. She'd been kidding herself, and now she was feeling the sting of it all along the side of her face.

"Go get a cloth from the galley. You're bleeding."

Leland gave Quinn a sideways look, so as not to make direct eye contact or any other perceived threatening posture. She replaced the dark glasses that had been knocked from her face, stood slowly, and walked back to the rear of the cabin and came back with a damp cloth. Holding the cool cloth against her lip soothed the aching just a little.

Leland had no idea where they were going, but even she could sense they were descending. Out the window she glimpsed red rock cliffs surrounded by a barren, ragged, desolate landscape.

Quinn must have sensed that Leland wasn't going to put up a fight because after a little while she got up and moved to the cockpit. She could hear them talking, but she couldn't make out what they were saying. Quinn moved back to the narrow passageway between the cockpit and the main compartment.

Leland could see the ground rushing past not too far below them. Wherever it was Quinn was taking them, they were almost there. Geography had been a favorite subject in college so she knew enough about topography, direction, and their flight time from CCSF to surmise that they were landing somewhere in the desert southwest of the North American continent. The question was, why?

The aircraft's forward motion slowed. They hovered briefly before the transport settled onto the ground.

"That's it. You're done. Grab your gear." Quinn barked orders at Ava who seemed to be lingering in the cockpit area.

As Ava moved past Quinn in the narrow passage, Quinn shoved her. Ava stumbled and fell against one of the seats near Leland.

"Nice try, Cap." Quinn stepped into the cockpit for a second and then rejoined them. "You didn't think I'd notice you triggered the distress beacon? How dim do you think I am?" She motioned with the gun toward the aircraft door. "Open it."

The interior emergency release was stiff, but Ava managed it, and the handle rotated twice into the open position. The door's seal released, and compressed cooled air hissed as it joined with the dry hot air outside. Leland was thankful for her dark glasses as the door swung away and the unfiltered sun forced Ava to shield her eyes. Then Ava hit the switch to lower the gangway stairs.

As the dust settled, it was apparent they weren't alone. A large group of people, backlit from the late afternoon sun behind them, fanned out in an arc between the aircraft and what looked like the entrance to an underground tunnel.

Leland had her small overnight suitcase in her hand, and Ava's gear bag was over her shoulder. As Ava adjusted the strap across her chest, she gave Leland a sideways glance, which Leland wasn't sure how to interpret.

"Move." Quinn shoved Leland.

A man and a woman stepped away from those gathered and approached.

"Take them inside while I secure the aircraft." Quinn handed one of the side arms to the man. He nodded toward the large, dark entrance just in front of them.

Those that had been watching parted to let them pass. No one spoke. Leland scanned their faces to try to get some idea of who the group was, but it was impossible to know. At a quick surface glance, they appeared to have no defining feature that united them. They seemed to represent several ethnic groups and varied in age, although she did note that there were no children among them.

Once inside, Leland had to remove her dark glasses or she would have stumbled. There were lights along the ceiling of the tunnel above them, but after the intensity of the sunlight outside, the interior seemed practically dark. They followed the woman farther along the underground corridor, past doors, past an open room with tables, all the while the man with the gun followed close behind them.

They were finally ushered into a rather sterile room with no windows. The door clicked shut behind them.

Ava checked the handle. "It's locked."

Leland scanned the room. Two narrow beds, a sink, small cabinet, a tiny corner room that had a shower and toilet. Low wattage lights were sunk into the walls around the room. She dropped her bag on the floor.

Ava dropped her bag onto the bunk along the far wall. "What do you think they want?"

"I'm afraid to guess." Those were the first words Leland had spoken since Quinn had pointed the gun at her head. She felt oddly distant from the sound of her own voice, as if someone else had spoken the words from the end of a long dark tunnel.

Ava was just about to sit down when the door opened and four people joined them. One of them was the woman Ava had seen in the museum in CC Amsterdam.

"You." Ava could hardly believe her eyes. "I know you."

"Do you?" The woman flipped her long, wavy silver hair over her shoulder and smiled at Ava. "I don't actually believe we've been formally introduced. I'm Meredith. But I do know who you are, Ava."

"How…"

"So many questions I imagine, but I must attend to a more pressing matter before I answer them." She stepped a little closer to Leland. Close enough to begin to undress her. Leland didn't resist as Meredith slipped the jacket from her shoulders and swept it down her arms, letting it fall to the floor. Then Meredith nodded to the man closest to her, and he proceeded to bind Leland's hands.

Ava made a move to intervene, but the two women standing nearest her held her fast; one on each side, they pulled her back to the far corner of the room. She watched as the man pulled a rope between her bound hands, threw it over a pipe in the ceiling, and pulled the rope taut so that Leland's feet barely touched the floor.

Rage surged in Ava's chest, and she fought against her captors. She couldn't get to Leland so she lashed out with words. "Fuck you!"

Meredith turned to face her, and the corner of her mouth tweaked up just enough to be a smile. "If you wish." She stepped closer to Ava and trailed her fingertip along Ava's jawline. Ava jerked her head away. "You are beautiful, but you will have to wait your turn."

Meredith returned her attention to Leland. Panic was spreading through Ava's system like a spider web. She was afraid of what Meredith was about to do, and she was powerless to stop it. She fought against the two women holding her to no avail.

Meredith slowly ran her open palms up and down Leland's suspended body. She fished a small black notebook out of Leland's pocket and shoved it into the back pocket of her military style pants. She reached deep into Leland's other pocket and pulled something else out and examined it. Ava couldn't see the object from where she was, but whatever it was, Meredith allowed Leland to keep it. She was smiling as she took a step back and looked into Leland's eyes.

"Now, where is it, Ms. Argosy?" Meredith asked as she slowly circled Leland.

Leland didn't respond. Her eyes were closed, and Ava could see that she was clenching her jaw. The man holding Leland suspended handed over some sort of metallic paddle-shaped device to Meredith. She began to incrementally trace the shape of Leland's body until the device began to ping rapidly.

"Ah, there it is." Meredith pulled a knife from a sheath on her belt. The blade was probably four or five inches long. She lifted up Leland's shirt just above her hip. The blade caught the light and flashed as she tilted it toward Leland's exposed flesh. Leland arched away as the blade sank into her side. Meredith wrapped an arm around her waist to hold her fast while she made the cut.

Leland endured the cut, but it was Ava who cried out. "Stop! What are you doing?"

Blood streamed from Leland's side as Meredith showed Ava the bloodied miniscule device in her palm. "Proof of life and too easy to track."

She nodded toward the man, and he let the rope drop. Leland's hands fell, and he untied her wrists. She seemed traumatized, as she stood silent and motionless in the center of the room. Ava fought against the two women that had been holding her only to have them shove her backward toward the bed as they quickly left the room with the others. Ava and Leland were alone again.

Ava snapped into action. She pulled a small towel from the cabinet near the sink, dampened it under the faucet, and pressed it to the wound on Leland's side. "Sit down."

Leland seemed as if she might be in shock. As Ava applied pressure to stop the bleeding, she scanned the room again and noticed a med kit under the sink. "Here, hold this. Put pressure on it while I get that medical kit." She pulled the kit free and returned to Leland.

"Lie down on your side so that I can see the cut better." Ava helped Leland sink onto the bed. The cut was shallow but still bleeding. "More pressure." She placed Leland's hand over the towel as she rifled in the box for supplies.

She pulled out a large rectangular sealed package of second skin and some antibiotic cream. She wiped at the cut, applied the cream, and then sealed the wound with the adhesive second skin bandage.

"Thank you." Leland's voice was barely audible.

"Hey, the cut isn't deep. I think it'll be okay." Ava reached to brush strands of damp hair off Leland's forehead. "How does your cheek feel?" A bruise was developing where Quinn had punched her.

Leland smiled weakly. "It hurts. How are you feeling?"

Ava stood and began to pace, chewing her bottom lip.

"Ava, I'm so sorry. If I hadn't specifically asked for you then you wouldn't even be here now."

"But you would. And I wouldn't even know it." She wanted to add *because I was too much of a coward to leave my number when I left you in Easton.* But she stopped herself. "Quinn is the one who got us into this." Fucking Quinn.

"How well do you know Quinn?"

"Apparently, not well at all."

They were quiet for a few minutes. She stopped pacing and looked at Leland. "What did Meredith cut out of your side?"

"A personal location device. All the ruling families have them."

"So now no one can track us using that?"

"Assuming Meredith destroyed it, yes, that's correct."

"And I was only able to trigger the distress beacon for about twenty seconds before Quinn switched it off. Not long, but long enough to register a location, if someone was paying any attention to our flight path. Which I assume they were."

Leland leaned forward, swept her hands through her hair, then rested her elbows on her knees and studied the floor. "This is not how I envisioned our second date."

Leland spoke softly, and it settled Ava's frantic thoughts just a little.

"I had this image in my head of how things might go." Leland propped herself up gingerly with her back against the wall, still seated on the bed. "You'd be surprised to see me, but happy. And I'd ask you to have dinner with me when we reached the cloud city of Miami." She paused and closed her eyes, then opened them again, smiled at Ava, and continued to talk softly. "And then maybe I'd convince you to stay for the weekend when we reached Paris."

Ava was touched by how far Leland had projected their second encounter. She sat on the bed across from Leland, facing her. "I don't know what to say."

"You don't have to say anything. It was my fantasy and now it's ruined." Just then, the lights blinked and went dark.

A faint, low light, barely as bright as a night-light along the floor in the corner of the room flickered on so that they weren't in complete darkness, but in the nearly dark room the walls began to close in for Ava. She looked at her hands in her lap and tried not to focus on the fact that they were trapped in a small underground room.

The more she tried to redirect her thoughts the tighter her chest felt. She lay down on the bed and covered her face with her hands.

"Ava?"

She didn't answer. She was struggling not to spiral. She unzipped her flight suit because she felt like she couldn't breathe. The realization that she was locked in an underground room pressed down on her and forced the air from her lungs.

"Ava? What's wrong?"

The bed shifted as Leland sat down beside her in the darkened room.

"Hey, what's going on?" Leland tried to pull her hand away from her face.

"I'm…I'm claustrophobic." Ava's breathing was rapid and shallow. Blood was pounding in her head. She felt Leland shift beside her.

"Listen to my voice." Leland placed the palm of her hand in the opening of Ava's flight suit. Ava could feel the warmth of Leland's touch through her thin undershirt. "Listen to my voice."

Leland was lying beside Ava now, speaking softly, close to her ear. Ava could feel Leland's breath stir her hair as she spoke. "Keep your eyes closed and imagine we're standing on the Golden Gate Bridge. You've been there, right?"

Ava nodded and tried to swallow around the knot in her throat.

"It's three in the morning, and no one is on the bridge expanse except us. It's very dark, but the darkness isn't small; the darkness is large. The darkness is infinite so that we have all the space we need. And you could walk away if you wanted to, but you'd rather stay." Leland caressed Ava's chest, moving her fingers gently as she spoke. "Breathe in...breathe out...now in again...slow, easy...there's no urgency and there's plenty of space here." Leland tenderly kissed Ava's temple. "There's all the space in the world, but we prefer to be close, that's what's happening now. And there's no reason to fear this closeness."

"Leland," Ava whispered.

"I'm right here with you."

"Thank you." Ava began to relax next to Leland's body. Her caress was nurturing. The warmth of Leland's hand on her skin just above her undershirt made her flesh tingle.

"Just rest." Leland kissed her hair. "I'll stay here with you if that's okay."

"Yes." Ava kept her eyes closed and focused all her attention on the sensations of Leland's nearness and none of her attention on the locked door of the small room. In the darkness she listened for the soft sounds of Leland's calm breathing and regretted, not for the first time, how she'd handled things in Easton.

CHAPTER SIXTEEN

Beck exited the central transit station in Easton and headed toward Jenna Bookman's brownstone. Freestanding dwellings were rare, but Jenna had married well. Her wife, Sophie's, family was very wealthy, and her parents had left the brownstone in Sophie's care. The building had been reconstructed based on a quaint vintage structure from Easton when it had been tucked into the rolling hills of the piedmont of North Carolina more than a century ago. The bricks themselves had been salvaged from a much older structure, probably three hundred years old. The effect was gorgeous. Beck paused to admire the exterior of the narrow, tall building. It was late so she was happy to see lights were still on inside.

She pressed the comm unit next to the door and waited.

"Hello?" Jenna's voice came through the speaker.

"Jenna, it's me, Beck."

There was a moment of silence from the speaker before the door opened. Jenna couldn't mask the surprise on her face. "Beck, it's about damn time you stopped by."

"It's nice to see you too." Beck stepped past her into the entry hall. "Did I wake you? Is Sophie here?"

"No and no." Jenna pushed the door closed. "Sophie's out helping a friend celebrate her birthday. I just got in from a late flight." Jenna motioned for them to move farther into the house. "Can I get you a drink?"

"Yeah, that'd be great. Thanks."

Jenna stepped to a bar in the study and poured them drinks. She knew what Beck liked so she didn't even have to ask. "You look good, Beck. You should have called me. I'd have gotten us some food delivered or something."

"Yeah, sorry for the short notice." She settled into an overstuffed chair next to an imitation fire, set ablaze in the replica fireplace. The blaze looked real, but there was no heat from it. Even still, the warm light of the orange flame added a pleasant ambiance to the study appointed with vintage furniture and fixtures.

Jenna handed her a small glass with scotch and sank into the chair opposite Beck.

"Is now when I get to give you a hard time for not calling sooner? You've been in Easton six months and this is the first time I've seen you."

"Sorry, I know. I'm lame, what can I say." Beck had only been in the house for five minutes and had already apologized twice.

"You're a workaholic."

"I know. I'll do better."

"Okay, so what's up? What brings you here at this inappropriately late hour."

"I need your help." She accessed an image file on the tablet she pulled from her briefcase. "I believe you know this woman." She handed the tablet to Jenna.

"That's Ava Wynne. I'm sure you already know what my connection to her is."

Jenna's tone had an edge to it, and she really couldn't blame her. Beck had asked a question she already knew the answer to. She hadn't meant to annoy Jenna. Her style of questioning was a habit from working at the Bureau. It wasn't that she had any doubts that Jenna would be honest with her.

"Sorry. I'll get right to the point. An aircraft Ava was piloting has disappeared. Chancellor Argosy's daughter was on that plane." She watched Jenna's expression change from curious to surprise.

"What?"

"A few hours ago, we received a distress signal. Do you mind if I spread this out on the desk?" Beck pulled a topographic map from her case.

"Please." Jenna followed her to the desk and cleared a space so Beck could spread the map out.

"The first signal we received was here. It only lasted for about twenty seconds." Beck indicated the spot on the map and then moved to a point approximately forty miles west. "We picked up the personal location beacon for Leland Argosy here. That position hasn't changed, so our assumption is they ditched the aircraft and traveled to this spot by some other means."

Beck pulled up images on the tablet again. "There's more." She handed the tablet to Jenna. "This security feed shows Ava leaving a bar in CC Easton with Leland less than a week ago." She reached over and swiped the tablet to reveal the next two photos, paired side by side. "This photo was taken two days later. I pulled it from the security feed in a museum in Amsterdam. That is Ava Wynne, and less than five minutes later, this photo was taken. The hooded figure is believed to be Meredith. The leader of the Return to Earth insurgency."

"What are you getting at?" Jenna's tone signaled impatience.

"And less than an hour later, this photo shows Ava at the restaurant where an assassination attempt was made on Chancellor Argosy."

"If you think Ava had anything to do with any of this you're mistaken." Beck could hear the defensiveness in Jenna's tone.

"And now she and Ms. Argosy are missing." Beck put the tablet on the table. "We know that last year Ava was reprimanded for transporting a doctor and an undocumented visitor to a community on the ground during the bombing on CC Easton and subsequently put on probationary flight restriction for three months."

"That was a private matter and had nothing to do with the insurgency."

"I'm simply giving you the data I've collected thus far."

"All circumstantial. Listen, I know Ava Wynne. She's true-blue."

Beck didn't miss the reference to the flight academy uniform color.

"Who was the other pilot on this flight?" Jenna asked.

"Lana Quinn, but she's clean. We checked her out also as soon as the flight went down."

"Well, something isn't adding up because there's no way Ava would do what you're suspecting her of. No way. I'd bet my life on it."

"I'm hoping you'll help me prove you're right." Beck shifted her stance and took a sip of her drink. "I actually believe you. This evidence is too perfect, as if it's being fed to us to throw us off from coming to some other conclusion." Jenna seemed to visibly relax as Beck spoke. The trail was too perfect and Beck hadn't been able to shake what the shooter had said to her in Amsterdam about a diversion. Was the kidnapping the diversion?

"So why are you here, Beck? Other than for free booze and to try to piss me off."

Beck smiled. "The chancellor wants to attempt a quiet rescue. His cabinet doesn't want this news leaking to the press because they feel it gives too much power to the Return to Earth movement. He's tasked me with the rescue, and I'm hoping you'll help me. I need a pilot."

"What's your plan?"

"Is that a yes?"

"Of course the answer is yes." Jenna took a sip of her drink and gave Beck an intense direct gaze.

"The plan is that we set down here, a few clicks away from the hit we got on the personal locator beacon." She pointed to a valley, surrounded by cliffs on the topographic map. The area was labeled Valley of Fire. "Hopefully, we'll be able to extract the targets ourselves. I assume your certification is up to date?"

"I'm still fully certified. I go to the firing range once a month to exercise my demons."

"Good, I'm glad to hear you're keeping your demons in shape." Beck was amused as usual by Jenna's word play. She'd really missed Jenna. And if Beck was going into the Valley of Fire, then Jenna Bookman was the person she wanted watching her back. "Try to get a few hours sleep and meet me on the southwest flight deck at four a.m. The Bureau team is assembling gear and a small aircraft for us. I don't want any more time to go by than necessary before we're on the ground."

"Should we leave now?"

"Better if you get some rest so we're on top of our game." Beck refolded the map and stowed it in her case. "The location device would signal differently if Ms. Argosy were dead."

"Unless it's been removed."

"Let's hope that doesn't happen. We can only assume they are going to make some ransom demand, so they'll keep her alive. Our goal is to get her before that happens. Her father seemed unwell the last time I saw him. I don't want this situation to contribute to his fragile condition."

"And you're wrong about Ava. You'll know that when you meet her."

"I hope you're right." Beck finished her scotch. "I'll see you in the morning."

When they reached the door, Beck stopped and turned to face Jenna. "Hey, and this op is off the books. You can't say anything to Sophie."

"Understood."

"You'll call in to work with a case of the flu."

"That won't seem suspicious because it seems like everyone lately is coming down with it."

Beck stepped through the door but stopped when she heard Jenna say something.

"Did you say something?" asked Beck.

"I said, thanks for bringing me in on this."

"Thank you for saying yes. I need someone I really trust."

Jenna nodded and closed the door. Beck turned and headed toward the flight deck. She'd get some rest in the crew lounge and check in with Frank one more time before she left for the desert. She was too wound up to try to sleep for real. Frank would likely be pissed if he knew she was going on this op without him, but this had to be low profile, and he wasn't a pilot. So as far as Frank was concerned, she was taking a much-needed vacation.

Vacations were as rare as dinner dates. Beck made a mental note to add time off to her *get a life* list when she got back.

CHAPTER SEVENTEEN

A knock at the door woke Ava. In the comfort of Leland's arms, she'd managed to fall asleep despite her initial panic. When their visitor opened the door partially, the movement triggered the lights to flicker on.

"Excuse me, but Dr. Ray has asked that you join her for breakfast. I'll give you a little time to freshen up. Then I'll escort you to her quarters." The woman pulled the door closed.

First they'd been ushered to a locked room at gunpoint and now they were invited to breakfast? Ava rose up on her elbow as the door clicked shut.

Leland shifted beside her. She gingerly sat up, keeping her hand over the wound in her side.

"Does that seem odd to you?" Ava asked.

"I'm beginning to think we should make no assumptions about any of this."

"How do you feel?"

"Stiff, sore. I'll live." Leland gave her a weak smile.

Awkward was how Ava was feeling. They'd slept together again, but this time it had been platonic. Leland had talked her back from the edge of sheer panic, and she'd fallen asleep in her arms and it felt…good. Really good. How could a really good thing happen in the midst of complete disaster?

They took turns at the sink. Ava pulled a fresh shirt from her bag and stepped into the tiny shower closet to change. Obviously,

Leland had seen her without clothes, but somehow, because of the previous night's intimacy, she now felt self-conscious. Funny how a night without sex could end up being so much more intimate.

After they were both ready, Ava checked the door. To her surprise, it was now unlocked. They stepped into the hallway where the young woman was waiting to escort them to breakfast. She introduced herself as Faith Akenzua. She looked to be somewhere in her late thirties. She was attractive, curvy, in an athletic femme way, with rich dark brown skin and rivulets of black hair that framed her cheeks and touched her shoulders. Her clothes were casual—slacks, boots, a snug fitting black T-shirt.

Ava was on high alert as they moved through the underground settlement. She wanted to take in as much detail as possible in case it aided them later. Several people they passed were curious and stopped what they were doing to watch them. No one seemed the least bit aggressive. They passed a large dining room filled with long tables and chairs that was bustling with activity, and Ava swore she smelled coffee. Real coffee, like she'd had at Cole's place in the mountains after she'd left her downed aircraft for the safety of Cole's home.

The corridor now was at a slight incline, and the area around them seemed brighter. Ava guessed they were walking toward some parts of the structure that had windows above ground. As they walked, the air seemed warmed by the sunlight.

Faith stopped and motioned for them to step through a door she'd opened. She didn't follow them inside. Ava turned as the door shut behind them. Leland stood in front of her. She seemed oddly relaxed.

An older woman approached them from across the room. It appeared to be Meredith, and Ava took an involuntary step back, remembering what Meredith had done to Leland the night before. But as the woman neared, Ava could see that it wasn't her. Her facial structure matched Meredith's, and she had the same silver wavy hair, but it was shorter, cut above her collar, and curly wisps feathered her face. Where Meredith was leanly muscled, this woman had slightly softer curves. She extended her hand to Leland.

"Dr. Argosy, it's a great honor to meet you. I'm Dr. Maxine Ray."

"Dr. Ray, it is I who am honored to meet you." Leland accepted her hand and then clasped her other hand around their joined hands.

"Please, call me Maxine. And you must be Ava." Maxine turned to greet her similarly. "I want to apologize for your rather abrupt and possibly unsettling arrival last evening."

Ava was speechless. Unsettling? That was the understatement of the century. Leland had been assaulted by Quinn, and again by Meredith.

Maxine released Ava's hand and motioned for them to join her at a table already set with food and drinks. There was fresh fruit, grapes, sliced apples, bread, jam, and coffee. As they took seats, Maxine continued. "My twin sister is...well, let's just say her methods are very different from mine."

"Of course, Dr. Meredith Ray." Leland gave Ava a look that indicated she was figuring something out. Was Ava supposed to know who Meredith Ray was?

Wait, why did that name sound so familiar? Dr. Meredith Ray. Meredith Ray. Ava repeated the name in her head waiting for some recognition to surface and then it did. As quick as a match strike. Dr. Meredith Ray was a physicist who'd advanced nuclear fusion. Ava had studied some of her work in college. Meredith Ray had been instrumental in the advancement of the power systems that made the cloud cities run. She'd seen a photo of her, but this Meredith bore no resemblance to that Meredith. Or did she? The photos she'd seen had probably been taken thirty years ago or more. And as far as she'd known, that Meredith had been killed in an unfortunate explosion in her lab.

"The food looks very tempting," said Leland.

Ava was starving, too, but she waited quietly.

"Please, please, eat." Maxine waved her hand over the table. They filled their plates with a little from each bowl.

"You might want to go easy on the fruit." Ava didn't want to say too much in front of Maxine, but she knew that Leland's system was used to synthetic food. She was worried that raw fruit might make them sick at first.

"Quite right." Maxine sipped coffee. "You know this from your time in the mountains I suspect?"

How the hell did she know about that? Ava quirked her eyebrows.

Leland gave Ava a questioning look.

"It's a long story." Ava pulled a chunk of bread from the loaf, broke off small pieces, and ate them.

"I imagine the tests you've been doing have altered your system somewhat so that you'll be fine with this food." Maxine was talking to Leland now as if they were old friends.

"Dr. Ray, I must tell you that I'm not sure how you seem to know so much about Ava and me. Also, I'm confused about why you brought us here?" Ava had to give Leland credit for direct questioning. Maybe she would just let Leland do all the talking.

"Call me Maxine, please." She leaned back in her chair and smiled in Ava's direction. "Do you know that Dr. Leland Argosy is a world renowned biochemist?"

No, Ava didn't know. She was beginning to feel like she didn't know anything at all. Ava shook her head.

Maxine turned to Leland. "I need your help, and I believe that I can help you."

"If this is a scientific matter then why the violent abduction?" Leland wasn't pulling any punches.

"As I said, Meredith's methods are not mine. Half of what she does is for effect and intimidation."

"Well, it works." Ava hadn't meant to say the words aloud, but impulse got the better of her.

"Had I known what she'd planned I would have intervened," said Maxine.

Ava couldn't tell if Leland believed Maxine, but Ava wasn't convinced.

"Truthfully, I believe she wants to ransom you to your father. That was not at all what I intended when I asked if she could assist me in bringing you here. And I will not allow that to happen." She regarded Leland intently. "This is a negotiation that she and I are still navigating." Maxine leaned forward with her arms on the table. Her eyes almost sparkled. Under different circumstances, Maxine's warmth would have been irresistible, but Ava was having a hard time trusting her. "I assure you that you are not prisoners here."

"I'm sure you'll understand if I find that a bit disingenuous." Leland's tone was even, but firm. She looked directly at Maxine as she spoke. "You say Meredith's tactics are not your own, but you obviously know of her methods and to an extent, condone them, otherwise you would not tolerate her actions."

Ava was surprised by Leland's candor. Surprised and impressed. Regardless of their compromised position as captives, Leland clearly wasn't afraid to confront Maxine.

"There is some truth to what you're saying. I shouldn't tolerate Meredith's methods, because I do not condone them." Maxine looked down at the table and ran her fingers across the lines of her forehead. "Meredith is strong-willed. I'm not always a match for her, but I'm trying. I'm sure you understand how complicated family ties can be." She looked at Leland and smiled weakly.

"Complicated, but not insurmountable." Leland took a few small bites of food.

"In any case, I'm moving you to better quarters after breakfast, and you are free to roam where you choose in the compound." Maxine's tone lightened as she changed the subject.

"But we're not allowed to leave the compound?" asked Ava.

"I'm sorry, no, not at the moment. But I think once we talk you'll understand why." She relaxed again into her chair. "And anyway, you're in the desert. Travel by foot isn't prudent and you're miles from any other outpost. Our nearest neighbors are a thousand miles away in the territory of East Texas."

They were quiet as they ate. Ava noticed for the first time that all of the walls of the room they sat in were earthen. It looked like some sort of red clay. Sunlight streamed brightly through small square uncovered windows. Shutters were mounted on wood frames around each window on the inside, but they were open. The windows allowed Ava to see that the walls were very thick. The space was comfortably outfitted with a long couch, a desk, and there were two other doors off this main room, but she couldn't make out what they contained.

"How is it you know of the work I'm doing?" Leland had finished eating and was now leaning back, sipping her coffee.

"To say we have people at all levels in the cloud cities sounds like a cliché, but it's true. The current of discontent has many tributaries. People are willing to become involved for the greater good."

"You'll forgive me if I'm skeptical." Leland's tone was calm, but confident. She definitely wasn't afraid to speak her mind. Ava admired that trait.

"I welcome a healthy level of skepticism. Skepticism makes us better scientists. Let's just say that I've been able to review some of your data entries at the lab, and they seem, how can I say this, incomplete. Given your reputation, those gaps must have inspired you to do your own separate studies. That's the information I'm most interested in. And if I'm correct then I'm sure that data is not in the government sanctioned lab where it would be at risk for alterations. Even if your father is the ruling chancellor."

Ava had the urge to kick Leland under the table to keep her from saying anything more. They didn't know this woman. And Ava had no idea what research Leland and Maxine were alluding to, but it would be foolish for Leland to reveal too much. Luckily, Leland seemed to have the same inclination, because she didn't respond to the assertion.

"Dr. Ray, I'm sure you understand that I might be reluctant to share any data until I know more about your situation here, and frankly, how this information would be used." Leland sounded calm, firm, but not defensive. She was clearly used to dealing with stressful confrontations. She seemed completely composed.

"Of course, of course. I completely understand." Maxine smiled and the smile seemed genuine. "I think we're going to like each other, Dr. Argosy." She poured more coffee for herself. "Now please, help yourself to more food, and after we've eaten, I'll show both of you around."

CHAPTER EIGHTEEN

B eck adjusted the mic on her headset so that it was closer to her mouth. "Jenna, can you set us down over there?" She pointed to a low, flat surface shielded on three sides by striated red rock formations. A hundred miles out, Beck engaged the wave shielding on their small aircraft so that anyone on the ground with radar equipment would not be able to track the plane. It was a long shot that anyone on the ground had tech, but since she didn't know what she was flying into she wasn't taking any chances. Which meant they also had to stay out of visual range.

"Yeah, that should work." Jenna banked the small aircraft and initiated their descent.

They'd left the flight deck in CCE at just after four a.m. Their flight time to the desert had taken about four hours. They were flying a military issue small cargo craft, and Beck had the ground support team pack it with everything she could think of that they might possibly need. Pulse rifles, side arms, food, water, extra fuel cells, a portable transponder tower, camping gear, and a solar powered all terrain vehicle. They had enough gear for ten and there were only two of them. But if their efforts were successful, they'd be bringing three women back with them from the utter edge of the earth.

The desert had been abandoned to wind, sun, and sand more than one hundred and fifty years ago. Scientists had sounded alarms about the catastrophic effects of a two-degree increase in global temperature. The oil industry spent billions on lobbyists whose sole mission was to derail policies that might have lowered CO_2 emissions. Blinded by greed, world leaders decided to play out the two-degree experiment because they knew they were wealthy enough to rise above it, literally. Then came the three-degree experiment. Millions died from famine brought on by drought and disease.

The planet warmed, climate shifted, and drought forever claimed large sections of the central North American continent, extending far to the south into Mexico. The huge urban communities that had once existed in Arizona and Nevada had exhausted every drop of water that could be bought or carried by pipeline. Those fringe cities were the first to fail when the power grids collapsed and the elite clans rose to the clouds.

Now no one went to the desert. Nothing lived in the desert. Why would Ava bring Leland Argosy to the desert?

Jenna's movements in the seat beside her pulled Beck's thoughts back to the cockpit. Jenna was flipping switches to activate the landing pads. After another few minutes, they settled onto the ground. Dust rose in huge puffs around the aircraft as the hydrogen boosters exhaled one last time before shutting down. The droplets of water from the engine casings likely evaporated within seconds. Probably even before they dripped to the ground.

They exited the aircraft and looked around. To say the landscape was stunning was an understatement. Beck had never seen terrain so fascinating. Red rock cliffs flamed around them. This place looked like old NASA photos of Mars.

The blue of the sky contrasted against the orange red rock surrounding them in such a way that it seemed to recede to infinity, so clear was the cloudless sky.

And dry. God, was it dry. Beck started to speak and found she had no voice. She cleared her throat. "I think we have enough daylight to investigate the personal locator beacon site. What do you think?"

"We're about ten miles from that position. We should have plenty of daylight to get there and back." Jenna pulled on a baseball cap to shield her eyes. "Who knows, if we're lucky we'll be home for dinner in Easton."

"Fingers crossed. Come on. Let's unload the ATV." Beck started walking back toward the rear cargo door.

"And let's please remember where we parked the aircraft. I don't fancy a night in the open here."

"Lucky for you, I'm an excellent navigator." Beck engaged the hydraulic pistons, and the entire back panel of the craft slowly folded down to the ground like a ramp so that they could back the vehicle out from the cargo area.

"I guess that means I get to drive then." Jenna grinned.

"Some things never change."

"What can I say? I like to drive."

Beck had to smile. She knew Jenna liked to drive, and that included a lot more than just ATVs.

"What are you grinning about?" Jenna looked across at Beck as she stowed her gear behind the driver's seat.

"Nothing. I'm just glad you're here. I've missed you." She pulled her hair into a ponytail, twisted it, and then pulled it through the opening just above the clasp at the back of the cap she'd pulled on to shield her eyes. Then she shuffled through some smaller items in the first aid kit. "Please tell me someone thought to pack sunscreen. Yes, here it is." She applied some to her face and the exposed skin of her arms below the short-sleeved T-shirt she was wearing. Then she tossed the tube to Jenna. "You better put some on too. We're gonna cook out here."

"Yes, ma'am."

"I don't want to get into trouble by having to explain to Sophie how you got a sunburn."

By the clock, it was still early in the day, but by the sun, it was already extremely hot, intensely hot. As Jenna backed up the vehicle and turned west, Beck scanned the horizon, which shimmered in the heat like a reflection on water. They'd set down in a narrow valley. Red rock rose on both sides of the gorge like the ruins of old walls.

They exited the valley and drove out onto an enormous basin. Beck felt small and insignificant within the immensity of the landscape. From the cloud cities, with their climate controlled buildings and technological advancements, it was easy to feel as if humanity had mastered nature. But Beck knew that here, on the ground, in the desert, the balance of power had shifted. They were driving into an alien landscape across terrain they no longer knew. Separated for so many generations from the earth as to be strangers to her, and as strangers, ignorant. Having no understanding of her natural rhythms.

They rode in silence, dwarfed by the scarred landscape where enormous striated orange and red rock thrust up from the ground in a sea of sand, like giants adrift. The ATV whined and lurched across the sand as if it were a boat on the sea.

After a mile or so, the surface hardened. The sand washes gave way to hardened sandstone. They pressed on for another five miles before stopping for water. The ATV had a canvas top that shielded them from the worst of the sun's direct rays, but with every tilt, the sun invaded the cabin of the vehicle. Beck's arms were already pink from the exposure. She was thinking maybe they should have waited past the peak sun hours to venture out, but she was afraid to let more time go by before finding Leland Argosy.

She'd met Leland once at a formal state dinner where Beck had been assigned to oversee security. It had been a brief meeting, but she'd instantly liked Leland. She seemed clever, grounded, kind, not anything like Chancellor Argosy who sometimes seemed self-serving, aloof, and arrogant among other things. It was her job to answer to the chancellor, but Beck was really here for Leland.

They stood beside the vehicle. Beck scanned ahead with binoculars, then traded the binoculars with Jenna for a water bottle.

"If it stays this hot we're going to use every bit of water we brought." Beck replaced the cap. She felt as if she could have finished it off, but she was trying to pace herself. She was fairly certain that neither of them was physically prepared to endure the desert for very long, and she hoped Leland was somewhere safe. They climbed back in and continued for another four miles. Then they disembarked and Beck pulled out a receptor device with a telescoping handle. "We're close."

"That's a bad sign then because I don't see anything."

Beck took slow steps ahead of Jenna, moving the device back and forth slowly in front of her until the signal alarm started beeping rapidly. Beck handed the device to Jenna and knelt in the sand to retrieve a small glass jar partially submerged in loose soil. The tiny locator beacon was in the jar, covered with what looked like dried blood. Beck's stomach clenched as she revealed the find to Jenna.

"That's not good." Jenna moved closer, her shadow falling over the small jar in Beck's open hand.

"No, this isn't good. Whoever did this knew exactly what they were doing. They had to cut this out of her. They know who Leland is and they knew someone would come looking for her." Beck began to turn slowly, looking for tracks that would indicate a direction of departure. "Damn. Whoever brought this here left heading southeast. See those tracks?"

"I see them. A single vehicle, not very heavy." The path of the wheels was barely visible, and if they'd been a few hours longer in getting there might have been completely erased by the wind.

"Did I tell you that I met Leland Argosy once? I really liked her." Beck was still scanning the horizon.

"Well, I figured you weren't here because you're a big fan of the chancellor. Listen, it's not like either of us believed this would be so easy." Jenna put a hand on Beck's shoulder. "We'll find them. If Ava's with Leland I know she won't let anything happen to her."

"I hope you're right."

"I am right. Come on. We should head back to the aircraft and figure out our next move." She started walking toward the ATV. "We are definitely going to need more water if we stay out any longer."

CHAPTER NINETEEN

Ava had been quiet for most of the conversation over breakfast, and Leland was anxious to be alone with her to find out what she was thinking. But any private conversations would have to wait until after Maxine gave them a tour of the compound. Faith rejoined them as Maxine led them farther into the underground complex. Faith and Maxine seemed close, but Faith was at least fifteen years her junior, and the nature of their relationship was unclear.

They toured the dining hall where everyone shared communal meals. Maxine explained that the residents divided themselves into different smaller groups that focused on specific duties. Some were tasked with reclamation and salvage, finding materials that could be melted down, retrofitted, or otherwise recycled for various uses. Some were in charge of food preparation and dispersal; others were in charge of infrastructure, and they were responsible for keeping the lights on and the water running. Still another group was tasked with actually growing the food. This was the section of the compound that Maxine led them to last.

The room was mammoth. To even call it a room would have been only partially accurate. The nearest section of the warehouse-type cavern was fully covered and sunk partially into the ground. The farthest end of the space was open to the elements, protected from direct sunlight by large canvases that crisscrossed to form a semi-permeable ceiling.

Leland was fascinated. This cavern filled with plants was a botanist's dream. Rows and rows of teardrop shaped containers were stacked vertically and then positioned in long straight lines reaching to the opposite side of the gigantic room. Pipes ran the length of each row, mounted just below the ceiling, with drip lines feeding each separate teardrop shaped planter. Leland had seen a hydroponic greenhouse before, she had a tiny one herself to grow herbs, but she'd seen nothing of this scale.

A bee buzzed past Leland and she reflexively ducked. "Was that—?"

"A bee, yes." Maxine moved so that she was closer to where Leland was standing. "We've been fostering a bee community for quite some time. It's much easier than attempting to pollinate the plants by hand."

"This is amazing." Leland walked farther into the space, stopping from time to time for a closer look at the vegetation. The plants closest to her were labeled Echinacea, Ginseng, and Nettles. As she moved farther down she saw Ganoderma, a bitter mushroom also known as reishi that was believed to boost the immune system.

Leland stopped and looked back toward Maxine, Ava, and Faith. "I've been growing some of these same herbs myself."

"Have you been ingesting them also?"

"Yes." Leland walked back toward the group.

"Farther along these rows we have various vegetables and even fruit trees over there." Maxine pointed toward the far end of the large open-air space.

"Impressive," said Leland.

Then Maxine turned to speak directly to Ava, as if everyone but Ava knew what she was about to say. "The cloud cities are sick. Did you know that?"

Ava didn't respond.

"When plant reproduction is engineered, plants stop adapting. And we, humans, cease to benefit from their evolution."

Ava watched the expression on Leland's face darken. There was definitely something going on here that she didn't understand.

"What's she talking about?" Ava decided to direct her question to Leland.

"Plants in nature reproduce sexually. When they do, they adapt to their environment and those traits are passed along to the next generation of plants. Basically, they evolve. When we eat those plants we benefit from their adaptation."

"So?" Ava was confused as to why this would matter. They lived in cities separate from the ground where everything was controllable. Why did it matter what plants were doing or not doing? All the food was synthetic anyway, or like meat, cloned.

"For the last few decades, illnesses have been more destructive because we're no longer eating real food. People's immune systems have weakened over time. Also, fertility has become more and more complicated and difficult." Leland gave Ava a serious look.

"And you knew about this?" Ava wasn't upset. She simply wanted to know.

"I've suspected. And I've been testing samples in various cities to evaluate my theories."

"There is no place where nature truly submits." Maxine stepped between them and rubbed a leaf from one of the nearby plants between her fingers. "Would you agree with that, Dr. Argosy?"

"Yes, I would."

"And at this point, changes may be difficult to undo. There's a possibility that permanent genetic alterations to subsets of populations could be irreparable. And are now irreversible."

"Can someone say that in English?" Ava knew she wasn't stupid, but this discourse was a little over her head and she wanted to understand what was happening.

Faith spoke from behind them. "She's saying that everyone in the cities is vulnerable to sickness, and they will keep getting sicker and they don't even know it. The elite clans and the city populations that they rule over are one virulent flu bug away from total collapse."

"The human immune system needs to be able to distinguish between self and other in order to protect us from disease," Maxine explained. "Genetically modified food is created by breaking through the cell wall, by introducing a pathogen into the cell itself. We ingest these modified genes in our food, and our immune system becomes confused. It is unable to recognize the pathogens in the genetically modified substances in the food ingested from pathogens that are harmful. The pathogens that make us sick."

"If you knew all of this, Maxine, then why didn't you inform the urban populations?" Ava wasn't in the mood for a science lesson. She wanted to know what the hell was really going on and why people in the know weren't sounding alarms.

"I did attempt to share my findings." Maxine turned to face Ava, her tone calm, despite Ava's accusatory tone. "I acted against ferocious opposition to inform the ruling elite. But they would not hear it."

"Then why not talk to the press, take this information directly to the people?"

"You believe that the press is free? That information isn't tightly controlled just like every other commodity in the cloud cities?" Maxine crossed her arms in front of her chest. "Are you truly that naïve, Ava?"

Ava was silent. Maybe she was naïve.

"And you want to know what this community is?" Maxine swept her arms in an arc. "A false vacuum introduced by instability into the nothingness that was. I stepped in to tame that instability, to marshal its strength and use it to begin the establishment of a new world order...here. That's the root of the Return to Earth movement. People should know they have a choice, but the ruling elite want to insulate people from the truth because they ultimately need those beneath them economically to shore up their position, their way of life. When the cloud cities were established, the elite promised equity for all who rose with them, but in the end they simply reestablished the ground's caste system in the cloud cities. Just in a more subtle and palatable form."

Leland seemed to shift her stance uncomfortably. Ava reminded herself that Leland was a member of the ruling class. She was sure that Maxine's words probably struck a nerve.

"Well said, sister! If I weren't already here I'd be breaking ranks to join you." Meredith stepped toward the small group. Ava felt her stomach seize at the sight of her and instinctively took a protective step closer to Leland. They had not seen Meredith or Quinn since they'd arrived and Meredith had removed Leland's tracking device.

"Meredith, I was just showing our guests around the complex." Maxine seemed annoyed by the interruption.

"Well, I hope the tour is over. I need to speak with you. Also, there's a dust storm approaching. We should seal this area off in the next half hour."

Maxine nodded. "All right then. Ladies, I'm sorry to cut our discussion short. Faith will see you to your new quarters. We'll all need to stay underground until the storm passes." Maxine motioned for them to leave the large greenhouse area.

Ava cast a backward glance as they proceeded into the corridor. Maxine and Meredith seemed to be having a heated discussion, but they were too far away for Ava to make out what they were arguing about.

CHAPTER TWENTY

B eck noticed something strange as they pulled up beside the aircraft. "What is that?"

"What?" Jenna switched off the ignition.

"There. Due east. Is that—?"

"A dust storm." Jenna had pulled out the binoculars. "Holy shit. I've never seen anything like that. It's like a wall of churning brown dirt heading right for us."

"Well, we need to seal every opening then, especially the exhaust casings. This aircraft will be a dead stick if debris gets into the fusion system." She moved quickly to open the cargo bay again, and Jenna pulled the ATV inside.

For the next twenty minutes, as the wind continued to build, they hurried to seal every hatch and crevice on the plane's exterior. Jenna tried her best to create a makeshift buffer over the main compartment door in an attempt to shield it from the worst of the buildup of loose sand. By the time they climbed inside, visibility was terrible and they had to cover their noses and mouths with cloths. The storm arrived suddenly and with violent force.

This was a setback they didn't need. And now the tracks they'd seen would be lost forever. Beck leaned back against the bulkhead and sipped some water. "How long do you think this will last?"

The wind whistled loudly, and the sound of dust hitting the fuselage almost sounded like rushing water. "I have no idea. But those tracks will be gone for sure now."

"Yeah, I already thought of that."

"We could check out the site where the distress signal registered."

"I was thinking maybe we should go back to where we found the location device today and head southeast toward the distress beacon site. They've got to be somewhere in between those two positions."

"We can start at first light, assuming we don't have to spend too much time digging ourselves out tomorrow." Jenna cocked her head so that she could look out the darkening window beside her.

"Why don't we get some food? We can't heat it up in here, but I think we have some things we could eat cold. I only packed cooking gear for outdoors."

"Wow, you really know how to show a girl a good time." Jenna's tone was light.

They divided food packets between them and settled against opposite sides of the compartment to eat. The wind continued to howl outside, and every now and then a particularly heavy gust rocked their little ship.

"So, are you seeing anyone seriously these days?" Jenna asked.

Beck realized they probably hadn't spent any real time together in more than two years. How was time passing so quickly? "No, not since grad school."

"I always sort of thought you guys would get back together."

Maybe Beck had too. Maybe that's why she could never commit to anyone. "We were just too different ideologically." Beck thought back to those days. They'd had epic fights that devolved into mind-blowing sex, but in the end, they were too young and too immature to navigate their differences. "I did try to find her a couple of years ago."

"And?"

"She's either married and changed her name or she's...I don't know, off the grid."

"You've got skills and contacts in the Bureau. I'm sure you could have found her if you'd really wanted to."

"When my initial search didn't pan out I decided it was a sign to just let it go. I'm guessing she doesn't want to be found."

"Well, it's her loss. You're a catch, Beck. And I mean that sincerely."

"Thanks, you're good for a girl's ego, you know."

"I do my best." They both laughed.

Beck watched Jenna from across the compartment. They'd been close friends in college and after. Somehow they'd done a terrible job of staying in touch the past few years. She could blame her travel schedule and Jenna's, but she knew it was more than that. She'd been depressed and lonely, and she knew if she'd seen Jenna she'd have had to own that and explain what was going on. It was easier to spend time with friends who didn't know her quite as well, friends who wouldn't press her for more.

CHAPTER TWENTY-ONE

Leland followed Faith as she led them to their new quarters. The rooms were next to each other, partially submerged at one end, but the windows along the far wall were above ground. There were inner and outer wooden shutters mounted on each of the thick walled openings. Faith reached through each and closed the outer shutter and then latched the inner one. They did this in the room that Ava was to occupy, then Faith ushered Leland next door and did the same.

"You'll need to keep these closed until after the storm." Faith set the last latch.

"And how will I know when that is?" Having never experienced a dust storm, Leland wasn't sure.

"You'll know. Listen."

They were quiet for a moment ; the wind sounded fierce, and the shutters vibrated against their wooden frames.

Her question seemed stupid now. "Oh, yes, I see."

"The desert has its own rhythms. It's very different from what we all experienced in the cloud cities."

Leland wanted to ask Faith more. How did she find her way here? What was such a seemingly sane woman doing in an organization run by Meredith? But she sensed that Faith had somewhere else to be. She simply said thank you as Faith closed the door, leaving Leland alone.

She was debating going to Ava's room when she heard a soft knock. Ava had come to her first, and that made her heart flutter in her chest.

"Hi, I was just going to come find you." Leland held the door for Ava to enter. She leaned out and checked the hallway. No one was around. "I guess we really are free to come and go. No one seems to be watching our doors."

"That's small comfort considering our overall circumstances."

"Yeah, I have to agree." Leland hadn't really had a chance to examine her new space, but she was hoping it had running water. She'd been incredibly thirsty since they'd arrived.

The one-room living space had a partial wall that divided a sleeping area with a U-shaped kitchen, which was very primitive—a small stove with two electric heating coils, a small basin with a faucet, and open shelving that revealed a sampling of dishware. On the counter sat a bowl of fruit and vegetables and a loaf of unsliced bread under a glass dome cover. Leland reached for a glass and filled it from the sink. She studied the water before sampling it.

"The water seems fine. I tried it in my room also." Ava paced back and forth across the small space with her hands in her pockets. She was wearing loose trousers and a V-neck knit T-shirt. The fabric of the shirt pulled taut across her breasts, and the sleeves outlined her toned arms. Leland took another sip of water. Ava seemed upset while Leland was unabashedly savoring how beautiful she was.

"I want to know what you know." Ava's voice had an edge to it.

"What?" Leland felt as if Ava was accusing her of something.

"I could tell that some of what Maxine was saying to you struck a nerve. If we're going to get through this then I need to know what you know."

"Oh, yes, of course."

"I recognized Meredith's name too. But I thought she was killed a long time ago." Ava was still pacing, but turned to look at Leland.

"Obviously, she's not dead, although quite possibly she's unstable. But definitely not dead." Leland moved around the island in the kitchen and leaned against it to face Ava.

"But how could that be possible?"

"I don't know."

"And who's Maxine? You seemed to know her right away."

"I know of her work. She's a biochemist, like me, only brilliant. I'd go as far as to use the word genius." Leland took another long swallow of water.

"Sounded like she has a similar opinion of you."

Leland's cheeks felt suddenly warm at the compliment. She cleared her throat and averted her eyes. "I've been struggling to remember the details, but at some point she was accused of sedition and relieved of her rank at the Global Academy of Environmental Medicine. This happened maybe ten or fifteen years ago. I never knew what was at the root of that, but I'm starting to formulate a hypothesis."

"I'm anxious to hear it."

"Well, two decades ago, maybe longer, several studies suggested health risks associated with genetically modified food—including infertility, immune problems, accelerated aging, faulty insulin regulation, and changes in major organs and the gastrointestinal system."

"Were you looking into this also?"

"I was. I have been. I'm beginning to believe that synthetic and genetically modified foods can create unpredictable, hard to detect side effects, including allergies, toxins, new diseases, and nutritional problems. In my research I found that Dr. Maxine Ray had vehemently urged long-term safety studies, but was ignored and then her findings were ultimately discredited."

"What does all of this really mean? Are people sicker than they used to be? Oh, wait…the flu. Everyone seems to be getting it."

"Yes, with compromised immune systems, the urban populations would be extremely susceptible to new virulent pathogens." Leland remembered a brief remark that Maxine had made during breakfast. "What was Maxine saying about, how did she put it, your time in the mountains? What did she mean by that?"

"My small personal aircraft went down in the Blue Mountains several months ago. I spent a few days with a family there. One person in particular, Cole, she's who you reminded me of when we…that night in Easton."

"So you spent time on the ground?"

"Yes, Cole's family has a farm in the foothills of the mountains." Ava stopped pacing and gave Leland an intense look. "There are communities on the ground that are nothing like this. It's not the way we've been told it is on the ground. Not even close."

This discovery pulled Leland's hypothesis in a different direction. She had suspected that the crossover event in the spread of the virus had been introduced from contact with the ground. She just couldn't figure out how, and she wasn't quite ready to share that with Ava. She wished she could make some notes in the small notebook Meredith had taken from her.

"Why do you think Maxine wanted you to come here? And if she's so connected to informants in the cloud cities, why didn't she just get a message to you rather than asking Meredith to bring you here against your will? She must know her sister well enough to know that her methods wouldn't be pleasant."

"I don't know. There must be something about all of this we don't understand yet." Ava's questions were valid, and in truth, Leland didn't completely trust Maxine's motives. She needed more information.

"Did Meredith have some other plan for you that Maxine isn't even aware of? If Meredith's attempt on your father's life in Amsterdam had succeeded you would be chancellor right now."

Leland's stomach lurched. Ava was right. How could she have been so stupid? She hadn't even thought of this. Sometimes she was too close to a problem to solve it or too close to a scene to properly see it. Leland had been groomed for this transition for most of her life, and she had been planning on addressing her environmental concerns as soon as she assumed power. But what would Meredith gain by expediting Leland's ascension?

Ava realized right away that she should have tempered her remark. For a moment, Leland's expression shifted, and Ava couldn't help feeling that in that instant the weight of the world had settled on her shoulders. Ava felt a pang in her chest for Leland who seemed suddenly vulnerable to the burden of her station in life. Leland was staring into space as if she was focused on some invisible thing. Ava put her hands on Leland's arms. "Come on, sit down for a minute. I didn't mean to upset you."

"For someone who's supposed to be so smart, sometimes I'm really stupid." There was recrimination in Leland's voice.

"I shouldn't have just blurted that out about your father and the shooting. I should think before I speak. I'm sorry." She settled Leland on the side of the bed and sat next to her. She pulled Leland's hand to her lips and kissed the back of her fingers lightly. "You know I was there in Amsterdam, at the restaurant."

"You were?"

"I'm beginning to think that nothing that's happened in the past two weeks has been an accident. Even meeting you."

"Meeting you was the best thing that's happened to me in a long time."

"Me too," Ava whispered, her words barely audible above the howling of the wind just outside.

Small ridges of dust were gathering on the window ledge just under the closed shutter. The light in the room was dim, the air still. Leland leaned forward as if she meant to kiss Ava, but she stopped just short of making contact. Her lips were parted slightly as if she was about to whisper something.

Ava looked intently into Leland's eyes. She ran her fingers through the short hair at the back of Leland's neck before she pulled her close and kissed her. She'd wanted to kiss Leland in the galley the day before, but she'd never gotten the chance.

She let her hand drift down Leland's arm, to her thigh. Her libido threatened to take over so she broke the kiss. This was Leland Argosy. This wasn't someone she could sleep with and then walk away. Although, technically, she'd already done that, and now here they were. Whatever they were going to be for each other, whatever they were going to mean to each other, had to be deliberate, not accidental.

"I should go back to my room for a while." The look on Leland's face was an invitation she was choosing to ignore. She needed some time alone to think. Too much had happened in the last twenty-four hours, and Ava needed time to sort through it all. It would be too easy to lose herself in Leland. Even now, she wanted to make love to Leland so badly that it made her stomach ache.

She forced herself to stand up.

Leland held on to her hand, stopping her forward motion.

"Are you okay?" asked Leland.

"Yeah, I'm fine." Maybe that wasn't the most convincing answer. She turned back to face Leland and tried her best to be reassuring. "We're going to be okay. I promise."

After a lingering moment, Leland released her hand, and Ava went back to her own room.

Ava was alone with her thoughts as she paced back and forth across her room. She checked her comm unit for the hundredth time. No signal. They were in a complete dead zone. Either that or the signal was blocked in some way. Why did she expect this time to be different from the previous ninety-nine times she'd checked? Ava tossed the comm unit back into her bag and continued to pace. She wanted to be away from here. She wanted to escape.

The wind seemed louder now, pounding its assault against the outside wall. Or was that the pounding of her heart in her ears? She fell onto the narrow bed and covered her face with her hands. Leland had been visibly upset when she'd mentioned the shooting in Amsterdam. But rather than stay and comfort her, Ava had run back to the safety of her own room. She could kid herself by saying that was for Leland's good, but mostly she knew it was her own problem, her discomfort with needing someone, or someone needing her.

Obviously, Leland didn't have that same discomfort, because the first night they'd arrived, she'd talked Ava back from the edge of panic. Leland was plainly a better person than she was.

CHAPTER TWENTY-TWO

Several hours later, the wind had calmed. Leland felt groggy. She'd only meant to rest for a few minutes, but the sound of the roaring storm outside had lulled her to sleep. She pulled out her pocket watch and checked the time. Ten o'clock. Having rested unintentionally, she now had the urge to leave her room and walk around. She stopped at Ava's door but decided not to knock. Just because they'd been thrown into this situation didn't mean they were going to automatically be together, and it didn't mean that Ava wanted to spend every waking moment with her.

Leland very much wanted to walk outside for a better look at their surroundings. It seemed that the storm had passed so she followed the passageway past Ava's room until it intersected another corridor. She felt a slight breeze coming from the left and turned, following that tunnel until it opened to the outside.

It was fully dark and clear. Leland lingered at the opening of the corridor allowing her senses to adjust to the foreign landscape and her eyes to adjust to the darkness. She took a few steps away from the manufactured light from the interior space so that she could get a better view of the night sky. She'd never seen so many stars. She walked a little farther and tried to keep still while looking up, but she found that the sheer magnitude of the heavenly display was making her a little dizzy. She wondered if what she was seeing was the Milky Way.

"Amazing, isn't it?" Ava spoke softly. Leland had not even seen her in the darkness, even though she'd been standing only a few feet away.

"Yes." Leland shifted to stand closer to Ava, but she was still looking up.

"The sky is so clear and dark here that we can see the Milky Way with our naked eyes. Unbelievable." Ava pointed. "And see that? That's the Andromeda Galaxy."

"I don't know much about astronomy, beyond the most basic facts."

"It's a hobby of mine. Although, you can never see this from the cloud cities, too much artificial light there. Sometimes I get glimpses on long night flights from the cockpit. But nothing like this."

"Do you see any constellations that you recognize?" Leland wanted nothing more than to hear Ava talk. Ava seemed relaxed, and for a few minutes, it made Leland forget where they were and why they were here.

"That's Lyra. And see the brightest light at the top there? That's Vega, a very bright white star." Leland followed where Ava was pointing as Ava continued to talk. "In Greek mythology, Lyra represents the lyre of Orpheus. It was said to be the first lyre ever produced, and Orpheus's music was supposedly so great that even inanimate objects such as trees and rocks could be charmed by it."

"I've never heard that story before, but it's a beautiful myth. It makes me wonder if at any moment these rock cliffs around us will begin to shift and move." Leland scanned the sheer cliffs above them, silhouetted against the starry night.

"His music was also supposedly able to quell the voices of the dangerous sirens. The ones who sang tempting songs to the Argonauts."

Leland studied Ava's face, dimly lit from the corridor's ambient light. Was Ava using the story of the myth to send her some subtle message? Was she the siren and Ava the Argonaut?

Or was it the other way around? The expression on Ava's face was hard to read.

The absolute darkness of the landscape surrounded them. Dim light from the corridor cast a glow into the black expanse, but beyond the edge of its reach lay nothingness, as far as the eye could see.

Maxine had not exaggerated when she said they were far from any other outpost. The only lights visible were above their heads, light years away.

"I wish I knew what time it was."

"It's a little after ten o'clock." Leland responded while still looking up at the stars.

"How can you be so sure of the time?"

"I suppose I'm not, but I can tell you it's a little after ten o'clock in San Francisco." Leland pulled the watch from her pocket and held it in her open hand. Ava looked as if she'd seen a ghost. "It's…it's an antique analog time piece." Leland had no idea why seeing the watch had bothered Ava, but clearly it had.

"I know what it is." There was an edge to Ava's tone.

"Did I upset you in some way?"

"No, I know only one other person who carries a timepiece like that. I'm wondering if the universe is trying to tell me something."

"Cole?"

"Yeah." Ava hugged herself and shifted her stance beside Leland.

"It was a gift from my grandmother."

Ava responded with a weak smile.

Leland wanted to make things right. They'd had this magical moment and then somehow she'd changed that by showing Ava the watch. They stood in silence as Leland debated the best way to navigate the distance between them.

"I think I'll go back inside," said Ava.

Ava still seemed upset, and Leland wanted desperately not to be the cause of it. "Do you mind if I come with you?"

"What?"

"I was just thinking that maybe we should stay with each other." Leland knew that was a reach, but she didn't want to be alone and she didn't really think Ava needed to be alone either. Their best chance of getting through this was together.

Ava didn't respond immediately. Leland's stomach sank.

"I just thought that we're safer if we're together...that's all..."

"No, of course. You're probably right."

That wasn't exactly the level of excitement Leland was hoping for, but she'd take what she could get for now. She nodded and followed Ava back inside. They decided to stay in Ava's room and set about getting ready to sleep.

There was really no other furniture in the room except two small chairs so the only option was to sleep in the bed together. Stripped down to T-shirts and underwear, they lay next to each other. Ava spooned up against Leland, lightly making contact.

Now Leland was having second thoughts. There was no way she was going to be able to sleep with Ava so physically close. She willed her mind to think of other things. She even forced herself to count patterns of numbers in her head. A method she used sometimes at night when she was trying to reroute her brain to think of other things than her research.

Ava tried to relax next to Leland, but her senses were heightened. She became hyper aware of the slightest movement from Leland, the softest brush of warm flesh against hers, the sound of Leland breathing, the smell of her hair. Just relax. It wasn't as if they hadn't already slept together. So why was she fighting the desire to be close now?

Tentatively, she put her arm around Leland. Her fingers brushed over exposed skin at the hem of Leland's T-shirt. Her fingertips drifted around the edges of the bandage over the wound in Leland's side.

"Does it hurt?" Ava asked softly.

"No, I'd almost forgotten it."

Ava settled her open palm on the smooth skin of Leland's stomach. She tried not to breathe, she tried not to move, but the urge to make slow circles with her fingertips, brushing them over silky skin, was more than Ava could ignore.

After a few minutes, Leland covered Ava's hand with hers. Ava thought the movement was to still her fingers and stop her from moving, but instead, Leland guided Ava's hand down and under the waist of her panties.

Such a subtle movement, but desire flamed within Ava's chest. Her cheeks heated as Leland turned slightly to capture her mouth in a searing kiss.

Ava couldn't stop herself now. "Oh, Leland, you're so wet."

"It's you, Ava. You're driving me crazy. Please…"

Ava moved partially on top of Leland as she continued to explore with her fingers. Leland shoved her panties down a little to give Ava better access just as Ava pushed inside. She grasped a handful of Leland's hair and whispered, "I want you, too."

Leland slid her hand down between them and into Ava's underwear. Leland stroked Ava with her fingers as Ava moved on top of her, centered over her thigh.

"I want you inside." Ava pressed against Leland's hand, and Leland slipped her fingers inside as they continued to move against each other.

Ava was close, and she wanted Leland to come with her. She felt Leland tighten around her fingers. "That's it. Come with me. Come with me, Leland. Oh, God…"

The orgasm pulsed through Ava. She was dimly aware of Leland shuddering beneath her. They held each other tightly. Ava kissed Leland's face, her neck, her lips, but she didn't move her fingers from inside. She didn't want to break the connection between them.

Leland smiled up at her. "Maybe we should try that again, with less clothes."

Ava laughed softly. "Sorry, I got a little carried away."

"No, you didn't." Leland kissed her. "You did exactly what I wanted you to do."

Ava reluctantly pulled away from Leland. She rocked back, partially sitting up so that she could pull off her shirt and then her underwear. She watched while Leland slipped out of her clothing as well. Leland reclined, and Ava just sat, looking at her beautiful, slender body. Her gaze must have made Leland uncomfortable because she reached to pull the covering over her, but Ava stopped her.

"No, don't." She moved so that she covered Leland with her body instead.

Leland felt so exposed under Ava's gaze. She was afraid that under too much scrutiny she wouldn't measure up. On a scale of one to ten, Ava was a solid twelve, gorgeous from head to toe. Leland had never been with someone as confident in bed as Ava. Ava seemed to know exactly what she wanted.

"Sorry, I was getting a little bashful." Leland kissed Ava lightly.

"I don't think you have any idea how incredible you are." Ava propped up on her elbow and brushed strands of dark hair from Leland's forehead. "Why didn't you tell me who you were that first night we met?"

Leland had been expecting this question, and she wasn't sure she had a great answer for it. "This will probably sound strange, but when you're a public figure people who've never met you feel as if they know you. They don't allow you to be who you are because they already have these preconceived ideas." Leland traced Ava's shoulder with her fingers. "Either that, or they just want to be close to you for status reasons, or for the money. It's just hard to know if people really like you for…you."

Ava kissed her before letting her continue.

"That night at the club, I just wanted to be me. I was so attracted to you and I wanted you to be drawn to me, for me." Leland became aware of Ava's thigh slipping between hers.

"Well, I was drawn to you. Even though I only asked you to dance on a dare."

"What?"

"My friend Sara dared me to ask you to dance."

"You're joking."

"No, see, you're not my usual type."

"Is this supposed to make me feel better or worse?" Leland wasn't sure if Ava was joking or serious.

"Let's just say that asking you to dance was the best decision I've made lately."

Leland felt herself relax a little.

"I'm fairly certain now that I've been dating all the wrong women."

"Is that so?" Leland couldn't help smiling as confidence notched up in her chest. She rolled Ava onto her back, slipping her hips between Ava's legs. She braced on her elbows over Ava. "I'd really like to make love to you."

"Yes," Ava whispered. "Please."

CHAPTER TWENTY-THREE

Ava felt something against her foot. Then she felt it again. She squinted and then jolted awake when she saw Quinn standing with her boot on the foot of the bed. Ava pulled the covering up as Leland stirred next to her.

"Good morning, Cap." Quinn moved her foot off the bottom of the bed. "Rise and shine. I guess now I know why your royal highness wasn't in her room when I checked."

"What the fuck do you want, Quinn?" Ava was instantly wide-awake, her rage granting her vivid visions of tackling Quinn and beating her to a bloody pulp. She'd prefer to get dressed first, but that wasn't a complete deal breaker.

"Meredith wanted me to bring you along for some reclamation work. You up for it?"

Leland was awake now but silent. Ava felt Leland's body stiffen next to hers.

"Fuck you, Quinn." Ava's response was low and throaty.

"Is that a yes?" Quinn leaned against the wall with her hands in the pockets of her loose fitting cargo pants.

"Yeah. Wait outside. I'll be with you in a minute." She might get the chance to pummel Quinn after all. This day was starting out well.

Quinn nodded, and Ava waited until she heard the door close before she got up and started looking for her clothing.

"Ava, don't go with her." Leland looked at her with a pleading expression, a slight bruise still visible on her cheek where Quinn had punched her. "I don't trust her."

"I don't trust her either. But she knows where our aircraft is, and until I find it there's no way we're getting out of here." Ava pulled on her clothes. She stepped into the small bathroom area and freshened up. When she came back, Leland was sitting up in bed, the blanket gathered at her waist, her hair tousled in that adorable, freshly fucked sort of way.

Ava's chest tightened unexpectedly. She did like Leland a lot, and she wanted nothing more than to climb back in bed with her and forget the world. She sat on the bed beside Leland and pulled her into a kiss. "Listen, I'll be careful. I promise."

Leland nodded. "Okay. I'm trusting you to keep your word."

She kissed Leland one more time, and then Ava flashed what she hoped was her most reassuring smile before she stepped out into the hall to meet Quinn.

Quinn started in on Ava immediately, as if they were still copilots, as if she hadn't hijacked their plane and stranded them in the desert. "So, first Leslie and now Ms. Argosy. I'd say you've got some mad seduction skills there, Cap."

Ava ignored the bait. "Where are we going?"

"Vegas. Did you ever hear of Las Vegas?"

The urge to punch Quinn came rushing back. "What?"

"But let's grab some chow first. We'll be quick and then we'll pick up an ATV and head out." Ava followed Quinn into the main dining area. They took some fruit and bread. Ava downed a quick coffee and then water before following Quinn out of the main entrance to the compound.

❖

Leland couldn't relax after Ava left her alone. Worry settled over her like a dark cumulous cloud. She dressed and went back to her room to freshen up. Once she was back in the hallway, she tried to remember the direction of the hydroponic garden. She thought she'd go back there and hopefully find Maxine and get some answers to questions that were gathering in her brain.

Following the central corridor led her to the main dining area where several people were still seated and some also milling about. Leland was trying to decide if it would be okay to get food when Faith walked up.

"Good morning." Faith looked different. She had what looked like a military issue cap on, with her hair pulled through the closure at the back. She had on cargo pants and a long sleeved lightweight shirt. Even still, her soft curves were evident. She looked as if she was going on some sort of expedition.

"Good morning."

"Have you eaten?" asked Faith.

"Um, no, I was just wondering about the protocol for that sort of thing."

"You join me as my guest; that's the protocol." Faith's smile was brilliantly contrasted against her dark brown complexion. She motioned for Leland to follow her.

"Thank you." Leland fell in behind Faith as they gathered several items from a counter near the front of the large room. Then Faith got coffee for them both. They settled into two seats at a long table near the back of the dining area.

"Where is Ava?"

"Quinn asked her to go on a, what was it she called it? A reclamation job. I'm not sure what that means." Leland broke off a piece of warm bread and chewed it slowly. It was delicious.

"That means I'll see her shortly then, because I'm with that detail today also."

"Will Ava be safe?" Leland regretted blurting out the question. She didn't even know Faith, but something about Faith's manner lead Leland to believe that she could trust her.

"I'll make sure she's safe." Faith reached across the table and covered Leland's hand with hers.

"Thank you." They ate in silence. Leland watched various people come and go. The population in this underground complex seemed quite diverse in both racial makeup and age.

"You know, I met you once."

That surprised Leland. "Really? I'm sorry. I don't remember."

"We were kids. Maybe ten years old. My father was the lead engineer for the cloud city of Cairo. You came with your father for a tour of the city's infrastructure." Faith took a few bites of something that looked like porridge. "You seemed really shy and you mostly kept your attention buried in a book you were carrying. But I remember you. You make an impression."

Leland felt sure she was blushing. She cleared her throat. "So, your father is part of the elite clan?"

"Was. He passed away a few years ago."

"I'm sorry." Leland had assumed the people here were from the working classes in the cities, but that was probably a stupid assumption. Now she had to know more. "How did you end up here, Faith?"

"Idealism. I was a political science major and was invited by a close friend to attend one of the underground meetings where Meredith was speaking. She pulled me in. Her energy, her vision, her fearless view of how the world could be."

Leland ate quietly, allowing Faith time to continue.

"I got involved with the movement because of Meredith. I stayed because of Maxine. I've been urging Maxine to break away." Faith lowered her voice. "We need to separate entirely from Meredith and form our own community. Our goals no longer mesh with hers, if they ever truly did in the first place."

Leland was surprised that Faith would confide so easily in her and fought the urge to say Meredith was insane. But why state the obvious? "Maxine is rather amazing. I admit I was hoping to find her this morning so that we could talk further."

"She's like the mother I never had. I admire her greatly. I've learned so much from her. I can take you to her before I leave if you like."

"Yes, thank you." Leland sipped her coffee, having finished most of the food she'd selected. Some of it she'd eaten without being quite sure what it was, but so far, everything tasted okay. Some of the textures were a little strange, but that was to be expected based on her urban diet of manufactured foods.

"Actually, we should go now if you're finished. It's later than I thought."

Leland nodded. "I'm ready whenever you are."

Chapter Twenty-four

B eck pushed against the door. It gave a little, but she still needed help.

"Jenna, I think this is going to take two of us."

They braced their shoulders against the door and shoved. As it swung slowly outward, sand spilled in through the opening. Luckily, dirt only came partway up the door. After a bit more effort, they had the hatch open and began to shovel sand away from the opening.

The sky was brilliantly blue and cloudless as if mocking the fact that the night before there'd been a turbulent sandstorm that blacked out the moon. She'd heard the wind die down some time around nine o'clock, but it would have been pointless to try to dig out in the dark so they had waited until the morning.

Beck was anxious to get back out and resume the search for Leland Argosy. They'd been on the ground almost eighteen hours and so far had very little to show for it.

She was just about to step outside with Jenna when she heard a message signal from the central console.

"Will you get the ATV ready while I check this incoming message?" Jenna nodded as Beck retreated back into the cockpit area of the aircraft.

After a few minutes, she joined Jenna at the back of the aircraft. Jenna had backed the ATV out and was loading gear into it.

"What's wrong?" Jenna stopped what she was doing and studied Beck's face.

"It's the chancellor. He's gravely ill."

"What does that mean?"

"It means we're running out of time. We need to find Leland."
Beck pulled dark glasses from her gear bag and put them on. "If
the chancellor dies without Leland back in the city, then there
will be a vacuum in the transfer of power. That's the last thing
we need."

"Even if she's back in time she can still be voted out by the
ruling viceroys."

"True, but in the short term she would be a stabilizing force.
Without Leland…well, let's not find out what happens without
her. Let's locate her."

"Let's get moving then. I think I have everything we'll need,
but maybe we should take some extra charges for the pulse rifles.
Since we don't know what we're going to find."

"Agreed." Beck climbed into the passenger seat.

"You're letting me drive again?" Jenna smiled broadly.

Ava waited near an ATV with Quinn. She'd watched as
several people loaded three solar powered vehicles with shovels,
tools, ropes, and a few cases of items she couldn't see well from
her vantage point.

After breakfast, she'd followed Quinn to a sizeable machine
holding area. There were three large bay doors that opened to the
outside. A couple of women and one man had been shoveling
sand away from the large openings so that they could easily pull
vehicles outside.

"What are you doing here, Quinn?"

"What do you mean?" Quinn slipped a long bladed knife
into a case clipped to her belt.

"I would've figured you'd be anywhere but here." Ava had
kept quiet as long as she could stand it. Being with Quinn was
making her skin crawl and her blood pressure edge upward.

"I can't leave. At the moment, I'm being held hostage along with the chancellor's daughter by a no-good insurgent pilot." Quinn sneered at Ava. She leaned against the side of the vehicle with her arms crossed.

"What? What the fuck are you talking about?" And then what Quinn had said started to gel in her brain. "You set this up! You're the one who brought the fucking plane down!" Ava stepped in front of Quinn.

"Yeah, but no one knows that. You're the pilot who's been on probation for taking an unlicensed citizen to the ground. Not me."

Numb disbelief passed across Ava like a shadow, followed quickly by shock. She hadn't stopped to think about how things might seem to someone from the outside. She grabbed the front of Quinn's shirt and pulled her away from the vehicle and shoved her. "You set me up!"

Quinn was obviously caught off guard because she almost fell, but she rallied. "Come on, Cap! You've been itching to get at me since day one on the tarmac in CCSF. Bring it!"

Ava swung at Quinn before the last word of challenge left her lips. She landed a solid blow to Quinn's jaw. Quinn staggered and then lunged at Ava, who ducked, launching Quinn over her shoulder and onto the dirt. A cloud of dust surrounded them as those who'd been loading gear stopped to watch the scuffle. Quinn was back on her feet, they circled each other with raised fists. Quinn swung and Ava ducked, then she delivered two quick lefts to Quinn's nose.

"Fuck!" Blood was streaming down Quinn's face.

"Not so easy when a woman hits back is it, Quinn?" Ava was still angry that Quinn had struck Leland.

"Stop!" Faith stepped into Ava's line of sight. "Both of you. Stop." Faith reached for Ava and pulled her back by the arm. "Not here, not now. This isn't worth it. Leave it be." Faith was talking to Ava in a hushed but insistent tone.

Ava's heart was pounding in her chest and in her ears. She was furious. She wanted to kill Quinn, but Faith was right. Now wasn't the time. She needed to find out where the aircraft was, and she still might need Quinn in some way, although the thought of needing Quinn in any way made her regret the breakfast she'd just eaten.

Faith pushed her back against the nearest vehicle. "Breathe. Breathe. Ava, look at me."

Ava fought through her rage to focus on Faith's voice.

"I told Leland I'd keep you safe. Don't make my job harder than it has to be. Quinn's not worth it. Do you hear me? She's an asshole."

Ava was taking deep breaths now, trying to calm down. She nodded.

Faith turned to address Quinn. "You're with the other crew, Quinn. Ava is with me."

Quinn didn't respond. She gave Ava a dark look as she wiped at the blood from her face with the palm of her hand.

"Get in." Faith pushed Ava toward the passenger seat.

Faith circled behind the vehicle and checked the gear before climbing in and slowly rolling the ATV out into the open. The cockpit was partially shaded by a canvas top, but there were no doors or windows. After the dimly lit interior, the sunlight was brutal. Faith handed Ava a pair of dark glasses. "Here, you're going to need these."

"Thanks." Ava sat in silence as Faith turned the vehicle west and they headed into what looked to be a vast nothingness. This was the first real look at their surroundings Ava had gotten. The terrain seemed like something from another world. Sandstone rock formations that looked more like works of art, no doubt shaped by eons of wind and sand.

"Where are we going?" Ava asked.

"To Las Vegas."

"That's what Quinn said. I thought she was kidding."

"We have to recycle and reclaim materials for the compound. In order to do that, we've been systematically searching the rubble and remains of Vegas for what we need. People pretty much left everything behind and the arid climate has basically preserved it."

"Where did everyone go?"

"We're not sure." Faith switched to a lower gear as they climbed a gradual long incline, and then the ATV bucked as it crested the sandstone ridge and dropped down the other side. "We think some of them may have been responsible for building the underground complex we now live in. Maybe that was their last effort to create a livable place here. But we're not sure."

"So Meredith's group didn't build the underground tunnels and rooms?"

"No, she just found them. Right after she found this." Faith pointed through the windshield. The most enormous solar farm she'd ever seen took Ava aback.

Spread out on the plateau beneath them, the solar mirrors looked like a shining lake broken into a million small reflective squares.

"This was part of the Crescent Dunes Solar Plant. It's where all our power comes from for the complex. The photovoltaic cells were still intact so we rerouted the power to the settlement. Actually, there's more power here than we can use."

"Wow."

"With Lake Mead for water and this complex for power, we really have everything we need."

"I hear a 'but' at the end of that." Ava looked over at Faith in the driver's seat. She seemed as if she was holding something back.

"But there are things I miss about the cloud cities."

"Yeah, like everything?"

Faith laughed. "Sometimes."

"How long have you been down here?"

"Four years or so."

"I can't picture you throwing in with Quinn and Meredith. You just seem different from them, if you don't mind me saying so. How did you end up here?"

"Funny, Leland asked me the same question this morning when I saw her." Faith tilted her head as if she were trying to figure something out. "I've been down here four years, but my involvement with the Return to Earth movement started back in college. I was idealistic, and at the time, Meredith was saying things that resonated with me."

Ava was silent, waiting for Faith to continue.

"Now that I'm older, I realize most of what Meredith espouses is empty rhetoric. She doesn't really want authentic change. She's just angry, bitter. She finds joy in tearing things down."

Ava thought of her friend Sara. She could easily have been swayed enough to follow a similar path had the explosions in CC Easton not happened. That catastrophic event had forced Sara to see Meredith's true intentions.

"Was Leland okay when you saw her earlier?"

Faith gave Ava a sideways look. "You like her, don't you?"

Ava didn't respond right away. Like seemed an inadequate word for what she'd been feeling for Leland. As they turned south and headed down a rocky ridge trail, she busied herself with the study of the solar farm in the distance.

"You don't have to say anything. It's obvious."

"Is it?" Ava asked.

"Yes, I could tell there was something between the two of you the first morning after you arrived."

"There is something." Ava wasn't sure how to describe it herself. They'd used the reason of mutual support and protection to spend the night together, but that had lasted all of a matter of minutes once they were lying next to each other. Ava found Leland to be irresistible.

CHAPTER TWENTY-FIVE

Leland shadowed Maxine for most of the morning. Now, they were having tea in Maxine's private quarters while Leland casually studied her small library of rare books. She had a lot questions, but she didn't want to overwhelm Maxine by asking them all at once.

As if reading her mind, Maxine spoke from across the small library. "You have questions?"

"So many questions." Leland turned to look at Maxine. She folded her arms in front of her to thwart the impulse she was feeling to take books off the shelf. She wasn't sure how fragile they were, although they seemed in good condition considering their age. Maybe the dry climate had less of an impact on their decline.

"We have plenty of time. Ask them."

"What did you hope to achieve by coming to the desert? By bringing people here?"

"I never intended to stay here as long as I have. I suppose initially I was looking for a sanctuary for myself and others who had similar beliefs."

"And what are those beliefs?" Leland was struck not for the first time by how Maxine seemed to blend language typically applied to religion with matters of science.

"I believe in the holiness of the natural world."

"I'm not sure I understand what you mean by that." Leland crossed the room and took a seat across from Maxine. A square, rough-hewn table separated them, and at the edge of it rested the small notebook Meredith had taken from her.

Maxine saw her notice the book. "I'm returning that to you. Meredith had no right to take it without your permission."

"Have you read the entries?" Leland still wasn't sure Maxine was the trustworthy person she hoped she was.

Maxine poured more tea for both of them and settled back in her chair. "I have not. It is yours to share when you feel ready to do so. Until then, I will wait."

Leland picked up the notebook and slid it into her pocket. She was comforted by its return.

"Thank you."

"You're welcome." Maxine smiled at Leland. They were quiet as they sipped the soothing tea. "It is illusion that humans imagine themselves above nature, or separate from it."

Leland wasn't sure if Maxine was talking to her directly or just musing to herself aloud.

"The elite worship a religion of progress, but that progress cannot continue indefinitely. It contains within it the seeds of its own demise." Maxine's expression grew serious.

Leland sat silently, contemplating Maxine's words.

"We need to create a new world order that reintegrates humanity into the natural world. And at the same time, create a more just society. A society that is not based on the worship of progress and profit."

"You're including me in that we?" Leland felt her stomach clench. She didn't necessarily disagree with anything that Maxine had said, but she also didn't know what establishing a new world order might involve. It would most certainly come at a great price.

"Yes, I'm including you in that we."

"I have a difficult time envisioning how such a change could happen." Leland was willing to play along with the concept for a moment and see where they ended up.

"Would you agree that society is currently not resilient?"

"I would." Leland harbored fears that urban populations were one major infectious outbreak away from a vast population die-off. Actually, she knew it was closer to a reality than a worrisome conjecture.

"We are at the point where in order to save humanity, extreme measures are required." Maxine leaned forward with an expression of earnest concern on her age-softened features. "If mere persuasion could dismantle our current cloud city societies or replace them with something better it would have done that by now."

Leland sipped her tea in silent contemplation.

"People love the idea of transformation, but sometimes they shy away from the personal sacrifices required to facilitate that transformation."

She needed time to think, so Leland attempted to redirect their conversation away from engineering the collapse of modern society to something more immediate and less cataclysmic.

"Can you tell me how you managed to grow so much food here? I know it's a bit of a subject change, but it's a question that's been nagging at me ever since we toured the hydroponic greenhouse."

Maxine smiled. "I understand that this is all a lot for you to process. So let's talk about the farm. We raided the Svalbard Global Seed Vault."

"Really? But how?"

"As you may or may not know, the seed vault was created to provide a safety net against accidental loss of biodiversity or in the event of a major global catastrophe. I think the current state of the world qualifies as both."

"I didn't know that site was even accessible, or frankly, that it even still existed."

"A Norwegian scientist, a close friend of mine, helped…" Maxine's voice broke with emotion, and Leland sensed there was some other aspect to this story that was much more personal.

Reflexively, she reached over to put a comforting hand on Maxine's knee. Maxine gave her a weak smile.

"Elaine and I were very much in love. She would have done anything to help me with what had become for me a crusade. She had access codes and coordinates. She made it possible for us to get what we needed to survive on the ground."

"What happened to her?"

"She succumbed to very aggressive lymphatic cancer shortly after we arrived here. That was more than ten years ago now."

"I'm so sorry."

"I was blessed to have the gift of true love in my life. I would never want to have missed that experience even to be spared the pain of losing it. Elaine was a brave woman, and I've done my best to deserve the faith she placed in me to see this through. To make the world a better place, not just for the people here, but everywhere." Maxine paused and looked at Leland intently. "I believe you can help me make this happen."

"I'm not sure I'm as strong as you think I am, Maxine. Or as brave." Even though she'd been trying to figure out how to convince her father that major changes would have to take place to heal the urban populations, she hadn't gotten as far as deciding how she would actually make him understand the urgency of the situation.

"At this stage in your life, you must know that you are not a sheep." Maxine placed her hand on Leland's forearm. "Leland, you are the shepherd."

"You think too much of me."

Maxine leaned back in her chair and studied Leland. "However it begins, each contemporary generation believes conditions in the world are getting worse. Whether it's the degeneration of society's moral fabric or catastrophic shifts in climate or fear of some larger impending unknown."

Leland shifted in her chair. She knew what Maxine was getting at. "I recognize that evidence of decay can be exhilarating, even mobilizing. History has shown us that."

"Exactly. Belief in some advancing ruin ironically sometimes finds its origins in faith, in the belief of salvation. That salvation can take many shapes, religious transformation, radical discipline, or revolution."

"That's a powerful word, revolution." Leland gripped the arm of her chair firmly to keep her hands from shaking. She bore the truth of Maxine's words, and they sent a tingling sensation up her arms to the small hairs at the back of her neck. She sensed Maxine was speaking from insights in her heart, some selfless desire to save the world, but the truth of the word made it no less terrifying.

"Yes, revolution."

CHAPTER TWENTY-SIX

A va studied their surroundings with fascination. The site where Vegas had been was now a collection of half-buried derelict structures, some surreal in their resemblance to ancient monuments. The Eiffel Tower, the Great Pyramid of Giza, and a replica of Lady Liberty lay partially submerged in sand. The surfaces of those same objects above ground were scarred and etched, having been exposed to the elements for a hundred years or more.

It was obvious that the ground colony had created a network of roads around the former city site. Certain structures had been partially excavated, and doors had been constructed that looked like entrances to old mining shafts.

Quinn's crew must have taken a quicker route. They passed them as they continued down the main thoroughfare, and Ava and Quinn exchanged glances. Just the sight of Quinn made Ava's blood pressure spike.

Faith took the next turn, and as they continued down the secondary route, Ava caught sight of her aircraft. The first floor of a very large concrete structure was open at the front, almost like a hangar on one of the flight decks of the cloud cities.

"Slow down." Ava touched Faith's arm.

"We can't stop here."

"But that's my plane." Ava also saw a smaller aircraft parked at the other end of the large space. As Faith continued to slowly move the ATV farther, Ava saw Meredith step from behind her plane. Now she could see that there were several women with Meredith all doing something near the aft cargo door. Large black coils of power cables ran into the open door to where both crafts were tethered.

"We can't stop there with Meredith on site." Ava could tell from Faith's tone that this wasn't open for discussion. Even though she'd only gotten a quick glance, at least knowing the aircraft's location helped ease her anxiety a bit.

She'd just crossed the first hurdle, locating the craft. As long as she knew where the plane was then the only remaining obstacle was getting Leland and herself to it. She tried to settle and focus on coming up with a plan.

"I saw a second aircraft in that hangar." Ava had assumed that she and Quinn were the only pilots on site, but that might not be the case.

"Meredith uses the smaller aircraft to come and go from the cloud cities. She has other pilots here if that's what you're wondering. And she has connections with the lower engineering decks in the cities."

"So that's how she does it. She's using service decks and entrances below the infrastructure levels." Ava remembered how Sara had told her the insurgents held secret meetings below street level. It made sense that those who worked in the guts of the city, where the turbine engines and the fusion reactors were located probably had a lot more to gain from a more equitable economic structure. It seemed that once a person was integrated down there they never returned to work on the surface, which definitely smacked of a caste system that urban dwellers liked to believe didn't exist.

They drove for a few more minutes, and when they were almost at the last structure before the desert's open landscape, Faith pulled off the rutted dirt path. "Here's where we get out."

"What are we looking for?"

"Copper wire and jumper pins. And any other electronic components that look usable."

"For what?"

"I'm not sure. Something Meredith needs."

"I thought you mostly assisted Maxine in the compound?"

"I do. Part of assisting Maxine is learning what Meredith is up to."

"Oh, I get it." Ava checked the flashlight Faith had just handed her before stepping into the darkened interior. "I'm a little surprised that Meredith is letting me come along with you on this little reconnaissance mission."

"She's arrogant enough to think there's nothing you can do to hinder her. And out here, in the middle of nowhere, she's probably right."

"That doesn't mean I won't try."

"Come on, this way." Faith clicked on her small flashlight and motioned for Ava to follow into the dark opening of the building.

As it turned out, they weren't on the first floor. Some of the flooring panels had given way on either side of the entry walkway so that Ava could see several stories down into the belly of the structure. Clearly, the lower floors had been swallowed by sand and debris after the collapse of the city.

CHAPTER TWENTY-SEVEN

Beck stepped out of the ATV and scanned the horizon with binoculars. They were getting close to the former site of Las Vegas, and the rubble was visible just ahead. To the naked eye, the dark shapes on the horizon would have looked like more rock formations, but with the magnification of the lenses it was obvious that what lay ahead were the partially decomposing skeletons of structures long ago abandoned to the elements.

She was scanning slowly when she saw something that was distinctly modern set slightly apart from one of the giant decaying edifices. Jenna must have sensed she'd found something because she was quick to ask.

"What did you just see?"

"An ATV vehicle not too different from the one we're driving."

"Do you see anyone with it?"

"No. We need to get closer. Come on."

They climbed back into the vehicle and dropped down the rise and headed across the dunes toward the northern edge of the ruined city.

Once Beck thought they were close enough, she directed Jenna to stop the vehicle behind a large dune. "We should go on foot from here. We'll be less visible without the wheels."

"Got it." Jenna pulled a pulse rifle from the back and slung the strap across her chest. Then she reached for two canteens of water and handed one to Beck, who was also adjusting her rifle strap.

They crossed the dry earth between the dune and the north wall of the crumbling structure without incident. Beck took the lead, easing around the corner of the building to get a better look at the entrance. Still no sign of anyone.

"They must be inside. Should we go in?" asked Jenna in a hushed voice.

"No. We still don't know enough, and I don't want us to be in a situation where we're outnumbered." Beck pulled something from the small pouch on her belt, checked the entrance again, and then darted for the ATV. She moved back to cover quickly.

"Come on, let's fall back. I put a tracker on the vehicle. That way we can trace them. If Leland isn't with them then I feel certain she'll be wherever it is they're headed."

They moved back to a position partway between where they'd left their ride and the half-buried steel and glass structure. They sunk behind some loose rock and waited. Luckily, the sun was moving west so that the shadow of the once tall building stretched in their direction offering them some respite from the heat and sun.

After about an hour, two figures appeared near the parked ATV. Beck took a look through the binoculars. She exhaled sharply.

"What now?" Jenna reached for the glasses. Beck sank down with her back to the rocks as Jenna took the binoculars. "Holy shit. Is that Faith?"

"Yeah."

Jenna sank to her knees and gave Beck a pained look before taking up the glasses again. "That's definitely Ava with her."

"Fuck." Beck uttered the word in a hoarse whisper.

"They're packing up. We should follow them."

Beck felt winded, as if someone had just punched her in the gut. "I need a minute." She'd looked for Faith. They hadn't seen each other since grad school. To run into her ex here, under these circumstances, left an impact crater in Beck's chest.

Politics had been one of the topics she and Faith had argued at length about when they'd been together. Beck always believed in the intrinsic good of the ruling class. Faith was distrustful of anyone in power, always giving credence to the conspiracies that circulated in academia. Beck was older now. She'd seen more of what humanity could do to itself and others. She wasn't nearly as hopeful or optimistic as she'd been in college. Her views had definitely shifted.

Not that she would broadcast her opinions at the Bureau, but Beck didn't necessarily disagree with parts of the message from the insurgents. The ruling class promised equity, but in the cloud cities they'd basically re-created a version of the wealth disparity that had existed long ago on the ground, just on a smaller scale. But that didn't mean she was going to follow a terrorist like Meredith, who just wanted to destroy society rather than help reform it. Change by force wasn't real change, and it wouldn't really solve anything.

This was the last place on the planet Beck had expected to find Faith. She'd assumed, obviously wrongly assumed, that Faith's views had evolved also and that she was happily married with kids somewhere, anywhere but here.

"Are you okay?" Jenna touched her arm. Beck realized she'd completely frozen in place, her mind running a million miles an hour ahead of her, sifting through regrets and what-ifs.

"Yeah, let's get back and check the tracker. We'll give them a head start and then follow."

CHAPTER TWENTY-EIGHT

It was almost sundown by the time Ava and Faith arrived back at the main compound. They had spent most of the afternoon raiding different decrepit buildings in the rubble of Vegas gathering components that Faith was going to deliver to Meredith.

Ava had hoped to get a closer look at her aircraft, but there were too many people around it as they passed by on their way back through the central part of the old city. Meredith didn't seem to be on site.

Leland wasn't in her quarters when Ava checked so she set out to find her. She was anxious to share what she'd learned and also to hear about Leland's day. She headed to where she thought the hydroponic greenhouse was, but no one she recognized was there. A few women seemed to be grooming plants and checking drip lines. They smiled in a friendly way at Ava, but didn't speak.

This whole compound confounded Ava. It seemed that the residents were divided into two groups. Those who where aligned with Maxine and those aligned with Meredith. Faith had confirmed as much during their drive back. With leadership split between two women who seemed ideologically opposed to each other, things had to come to a head soon. One could almost sense the tension in the air of an impending confrontation.

Ava wandered through a maze of corridors that seemed to be descending farther underground. The air was cooler and had the slightest hint of moisture. After a few more turns, Ava realized why. She stepped into a large underground cave that was completely full of water, almost like an underground lake. Only one person stood at the edge of the reservoir, Maxine. Her back was toward Ava, and for a moment Ava considered quietly leaving, but before she made up her mind to go, Maxine must have sensed her presence because she turned and motioned for Ava to join her at the water's edge.

As she got closer, Ava could see that the water was shallow, maybe only two or three feet deep and crystal clear. They stood near each other in silence. A large droplet of water fell from one of the overhead stalactites, sending a succession of ripples over the calm surface. Then a second drop, and those ripples intersected the others, then a third disturbed the formerly glassy surface.

The aquatic dance was mesmerizing, like watching a fluid Zen garden in motion.

"I find this to be very soothing." Maxine spoke softly, as if she were afraid the sound of her voice would still the motion of the terrestrial raindrops.

"It is hypnotic. Is this an underground lake?"

"Not exactly. It's more of a holding reservoir for water leached from Lake Mead. There is a pump at the other end that fills water tanks throughout the compound. It's not running right now, which is why the water is so still."

Ava stood quietly, watching more ripples appear as water dripped slowly from the ceiling in various spots around the large cavern. Ava had never been in a cave before. She'd seen photos in geology books in college. But all of that was merely conceptual if you never actually got to set foot on the ground.

"I sense that you do not yet trust me." Maxine didn't look at Ava as she spoke, and there was no hint of defensiveness in her tone.

Ava didn't respond. What could she say? It was true. She didn't trust Maxine or Meredith, although there was a soothing quality about Maxine's presence. But still, it was hard to trust anyone who was an accomplice to your captivity, even a passive accomplice.

"I know that Meredith has been stirring discontent in the cloud cities. And she has alienated many in this community as well who, like me, do not agree with her more violent tactics."

Ava waited for Maxine to continue. It had been her experience that if you kept quiet, others would fill the silence.

"For those in the cities who follow her, she offers some sense of purpose, some sense of meaning. For many here in this community, she offers action without any true resolution."

"Why are you telling me this?" Ava didn't really want to understand the philosophy behind all of this. She just wanted to find a way home.

"Because I want you to trust me. I'd like to go back to the cloud city with Leland, and I'll need a pilot to take us there."

Ava thought of Quinn. Maxine obviously didn't want to ask Quinn for some reason. "Where is Leland?"

"She's in my personal library. I believe she wanted some time alone to think."

"So you would leave the community here?" Ava wanted to add *under Meredith's control*, but she stopped herself.

"Ava, there's something much larger going on here, and I hope you'll be part of it. You've actually already participated in real change; you just don't know it yet." Maxine smiled at her.

That was cryptic and unsettling. What the hell did she mean by *real change*? Ava was getting tired of feeling as if she were in the dark every time she listened to Maxine talk. The first morning over breakfast, it was almost as if Maxine and Leland had some secret code they were speaking in.

Well, Ava was getting fed up with this little outpost of misfit scientists, and she wasn't going to spend a lot more time trying to solve Maxine's riddles. She was going to get back to her damn aircraft and get Leland to CCSF.

"If you'll excuse me, I'm going to go find Leland." Ava was done with this conversation. She wasn't about to get sucked into whatever scheme Maxine had for her.

"As you wish."

Ava had only traveled a hundred feet or so back up the main corridor when a tall figure approached. The figure was backlit against the glowing orbs mounted in the tunnel walls so the woman was almost next to Ava before she realized it was Meredith. She was sure she'd visibly flinched at the realization. Ava quickly stepped sideways to pass Meredith, but Meredith mimicked her movement to the side, blocking her. Ava took a step back. Meredith was taller than Ava. Given her intense demeanor and height, she was an intimidating woman. When Ava had seen Meredith in the museum in Amsterdam, she'd been unsettled by her concentrated gaze and this time was no different.

Ava moved to the other side to try to walk past Meredith, but again her passage was blocked.

"Ava." Meredith's tone was low, throaty.

This was the first time Ava had seen Meredith since she'd strung Leland up and cut into her tender flesh. Anger was bubbling up into Ava's chest cavity. She was having a hard time not allowing herself to act on it. She looked up at Meredith but didn't speak.

Meredith traced Ava's jaw with her fingertips in what Ava decided was a predatory fashion. Ava took a step back, and Meredith advanced, closing the space between them until Ava felt the rock wall of the tunnel against her back.

"What do you want?" Ava tried to sound calmer than she felt.

"So many things." It was almost a whisper.

Meredith was probably twenty-five years Ava's senior, but still a handsome woman. Where her twin, Maxine, was soft and maternal in demeanor, Meredith was lean and carried an air of ruthlessness. She wore her hair long and full like some Amazon warrior, her skin darkly tanned in contrast to her silver hair. If Ava didn't believe her to be dangerous and possibly insane, she'd have found her intriguing. As it was though, Meredith made her feel a bit like prey beneath the hungry gaze of an unpredictable predator.

Meredith pressed closer. Ava turned away and closed her eyes. She felt Meredith's breath against her face.

"Meredith?"

That was Quinn's voice, a few feet from where they were standing. Ava opened her eyes to see Quinn's dark gaze. She looked at Meredith like a jealous girlfriend. *Hmm, that was an unexpected twist, but not completely out of character.*

"Quinn?" Meredith said her name, but she didn't move away from Ava or look in Quinn's direction.

"You told me to find you when I'd done what you asked."

"Return to your quarters. I'll come to you when I've had a chance to speak with my sister." Meredith hadn't changed her position. She was still standing far too close to Ava for her comfort and was staring down at her with that penetrating gaze.

Ava glanced again at Quinn, who seemed reluctant to leave.

Finally, Meredith took a step back and looked in Quinn's direction. "Go."

Quinn slowly turned and walked back up the corridor toward the main living quarters and the dining area. After another few uncomfortable minutes under Meredith's scrutiny, she smiled at Ava. "Another time."

Ava watched Meredith turn and head toward the reservoir where she'd left Maxine. Only when she was completely out of sight did Ava allow herself to relax. She took several deep breaths in an attempt to shake off the encounter and then she followed Quinn's exit to look for Leland.

Chapter Twenty-nine

B eck and Jenna followed the trace signal until they lost it. There seemed to be a dead zone with some sort of interference. Beck decided they should continue in the same direction in hopes that they would find some sort of lead. As they topped a low rise, Beck saw movement ahead. Jenna had seen it too and reacted quickly by throwing the ATV in reverse. Once they were behind the crest of the hill, they killed the power and moved to the ridge on their knees. Beck took the first look with the binoculars and then handed them to Jenna.

"That looks like some sort of underground settlement."

"Yeah, and that seems to be the main entrance straight ahead. That has to be where they went." Jenna lowered the glasses. She was bracing on her elbows. They were lying side-by-side on their stomachs to stay out of sight.

"They must have some sort of security shield. That must be why we lost the signal."

"That would also explain why radar didn't pick this up. This was definitely not on your recon map."

"No, it wasn't." Beck took the binoculars again. "It's almost dark, so that'll give us cover, but do we have enough ammo for this? I was expecting a dozen at the most, but now we have no idea how many insurgents are in there."

"Without the tracking device and with Leland having no personal locator, we're going to be heading in there blind."

"What do you think our next step should be?" Beck should take the lead, but seeing Faith had shaken her up. She'd asked Jenna to come with her because she trusted her. She honestly wanted to hear Jenna's opinion about their options.

"Well, we have no idea how many people are in there or how well armed they are, if at all, and we have no idea where to start looking for Leland. Maybe we should watch for Ava. She's our best and only real lead." Jenna turned to face Beck. "We saw her outside today in the ATV; I'm guessing we'll see her again. We could grab her first and get more intel."

"That's assuming she's not involved in this kidnapping."

"I know she's not."

"When we saw her today she didn't look as if she was being compelled to do anything by force. She looked like a willing participant in whatever is going on."

"Beck, she was with Faith. I have to believe that there's something going on here we don't completely understand. I know Ava would never do what you think she's capable of…and the Faith I used to know wouldn't either."

Beck nodded. It was her job to think the worst, to look at every possible way something could go wrong. And it had been her experience that many times things did play out badly. And even sometimes when she tried to imagine the worst, she wasn't even close. "Okay. We wait a little longer. Let's move the ATV back so that we can camp nearby. Now that we've found this entrance I don't want to get too far away in case something changes."

"Agreed."

They crawled down from the ridge and started driving slowly back in the direction they'd just come.

"There, the GPS came back online. We must be just beyond the reach of their radar shield." Jenna had been watching the screen in the dash for the readout to come to life.

"We can camp behind those rocks over there, and I can access the ship's onboard computer from here. I want to find out if there have been any status updates while we've been out of range."

They wouldn't be able to build a fire or use much light for fear of being spotted, but they could cold camp. It would be a long night, but not the first of those that Beck had endured.

Jenna pulled out some food and two warming blankets. As the sun set, the temperature began to drop. The temperature swings in the desert from day to night were big.

Beck plugged her handheld comm unit into the ATV's system and waited for messages to download. She read the readout shaking her head.

"What's up?"

"The chancellor's condition has worsened." Beck sincerely hoped they could find Leland and get back to the city before it was too late.

"Where is he?"

"In CC Easton. He was there for the trade summit when he fell ill. All the viceroys are there, and apparently sessions have been temporarily suspended in hopes that his condition will improve."

Beck settled across from Jenna, leaning against the nearest rock. She pulled the blanket around her shoulders as she broke open a food bar and began to nibble at the edge of it. She didn't really feel hungry, but she knew she should eat to keep her strength up.

"Are you okay?" asked Jenna.

"You keep asking me that. And yes, I'm okay." Beck's tone had an edge to it that she hadn't really intended.

"I keep asking because I can tell you're not okay. I can see it on your face. I can hear it in your voice."

Beck dropped her hands to her lap and slumped back against the rock face. "I'm sorry."

"You don't have to talk about it, but if you want to, I'm here."

"I don't know what I'm feeling. This is the last place I expected to see Faith, and I realized when I saw her that, well,

I still have feelings for her." Beck put her head down on her forearm across her raised knees. "Damn. I don't want to have feelings about her one way or the other."

"Good luck with that."

"Shut up."

"You just need to feel what you feel, Beck. Don't beat yourself up for being human. You really loved Faith. Maybe you still do."

When Beck looked up, she felt a tear trail down her cheek against her will. "Why here? Why now?"

"Because it's the most inconvenient place and time. That's how love works."

"Well, I fucking hate love."

Jenna tried to squelch a laugh, but she couldn't.

"Don't laugh. It's not funny." Beck threw her protein bar at Jenna.

"Thanks. I was feeling pretty hungry." Jenna took a bite from it and then tossed it back.

Beck sighed and leaned her head back and closed her eyes. Why, why, why? Maybe she'd actually get answers tomorrow. Tomorrow needed to be the day they found Leland. Time was running out.

CHAPTER THIRTY

U nable to locate Leland after her encounter with Meredith, Ava went back to her quarters to shower. This had been a very long day, most of it spent in the dry heat of the desert. More than once Ava had wiped her forehead and found a white powder on her fingers. Salt. She'd been sweating, but the perspiration had evaporated in the arid climate, leaving only a salt residue behind.

The shower compartment was narrow and small. Ava stood under the water for longer than was usual. She'd cooled the water so that it was just below room temperature. Her head felt hot and her cheeks were flushed. Meredith had freaked her out a little, and a cold shower might cool her anger.

She put on fresh clothes and was just about to go look for Leland again when she heard a knock at the door. Ava opened it to find Leland carrying plates of food.

"I brought dinner, in case you haven't eaten."

"I haven't. Thank you. Please, come in." Ava held the door open for Leland who put the food on the counter in the small kitchen nook.

"How are you?" asked Leland.

"I'm…I'm okay."

"That didn't sound very convincing."

"I had a little run-in with Meredith. It's nothing. I'll shake it off."

"I spent a lot of time with Maxine today."

"I heard."

"Really?"

"Yeah, I ran into Maxine also after I came back from the scavenger hunt with Faith, when I was looking for you." Ava reached for a carrot.

"Here, sit, eat. We can talk while we eat." Leland pulled two stools up to the counter and took a seat.

"I think Maxine has plans she wants our help with," said Ava.

"You're right. She and I spoke about this earlier today."

"And?"

"I'm not sure what to do. I don't disagree with her. But to do what she's asking would be...extreme. Things would change drastically. And by things, I mean everything."

"I don't want things to change." Ava pushed food around on her plate, not looking up at Leland. "I like my life the way it is. I know some people in the cities aren't happy, but that's the human condition isn't it? There's no way to make everyone happy all the time."

"I think what Maxine is proposing is a new structure that gives everyone the same options. I don't think she believes you can make everyone happy either, but there's no doubt that the current system isn't really fair for all."

Ava looked intently at Leland. "She's gotten to you hasn't she?"

"What?"

"She's sucking you in. I thought you wanted to correct the problems with the food supply to stave off some looming epidemic."

"I do want to heal our food supply." Leland was beginning to feel as if she were under attack.

"Now Maxine has you talking about a revolt to overthrow some perceived caste system? Maxine needs you, Leland. You don't need her. She's using you."

"I know she needs my help, but that's because of my influence with my father. I don't believe she's using me. It doesn't feel like that to me."

"I think you're being naïve."

Leland bristled at Ava's criticism. Ava's body language seemed defensive, and Leland wondered why. Something had obviously happened earlier in the day, maybe during Ava's encounter with Meredith. She wasn't naïve; she didn't think for one minute that what Maxine was proposing would be easy. Ignoring Ava's remark about being naïve, Leland instead tried to get Ava to talk about what was really going on.

"What happened when you saw Meredith earlier?" Leland stopped eating and watched Ava.

"Nothing."

"Something happened. You seem upset."

"Why, because I said you're naïve? Don't make this about me." There was an angry edge to Ava's tone.

"Ava, talk to me. We're in this together." She reached over and touched Ava's arm. Ava visibly flinched, and that hurt more than Ava's defensive tone.

Ava stood and started to pace back and forth. Something was definitely troubling her. Leland debated going back to her room and leaving Ava to work through whatever this was on her own, but something told her that distance was not what Ava needed right now.

Leland stepped in front of her to halt the pacing. She held Ava's arms with her hands, forcing Ava to face her. She could tell Ava wanted to pull away, but she held fast. She pulled Ava close and cradled her head under her chin. At first, Ava's body was tense against hers. She made slow circles on Ava's back and stroked her head, her hair still damp from the shower.

"It's okay. Whatever it is, it's going to be okay. Nothing has to change unless you want it to," Leland whispered into Ava's hair.

She felt Ava's arms encircle her waist, slowly closing around her.

"I'm sorry." Ava's voice was full of emotion.

"Ava, whatever happens here, please don't let it come between us."

"What are you saying?"

Leland held Ava at arm's length so that she could see her face. It was time to speak her truth. "I'm trying to say that I'm falling for you."

It was hard to interpret the expression on Ava's face. The fact that she didn't respond right away to Leland's confession made a knot rise to her throat. She reminded herself that whatever she felt for Ava might not be reciprocated at the same level.

Technically, they hadn't spent very much time together, and all of it had been under rather extreme circumstances. But Leland knew that she'd felt something for Ava that first night they'd been together, something completely different from anything she'd ever felt before. That's why she'd requested Ava's flight crew for the trip to Miami. She knew she had to see Ava again.

But maybe she was the only one on this side of the equation feeling the things she was feeling.

Ava still hadn't spoken, but as if in slow motion, she reached up and grasped the hair at the back of Leland's head in her fingers and pulled her into a kiss. The kiss started slow, an exploration of soft touches, and then built in intensity. Ava was making love to her with this kiss, and after a few minutes, Leland was completely lost in it.

"Leland, I'm sorry I didn't respond right away. You caught me off guard."

"That's okay. You don't have to respond. Whatever you feel or don't feel won't change the truth of what I said—"

Ava covered Leland's mouth with her hand to get her to stop talking. "I am falling for you, too."

Warmth spread through Leland's entire body in response. Warmth and relief that she was not alone in feeling the way she was feeling. "I'll admit that you scared me a little when you didn't say something," said Leland softly.

"Can we just pretend we're somewhere else, anywhere else? I want to be with you." Ava pulled her shirt over her head in one quick motion and then her bra was next. Bare-chested, she pressed against Leland.

"Yes. Yes to everything. Yes to somewhere else. Yes to making love. Yes to you." Leland slowly traced the outside curve of Ava's breasts with her hands. "You are gorgeous. Fascinating. Exhilarating."

Ava pushed her backward toward the sleeping alcove. They quickly shed the rest of their clothing and then climbed onto the bed. Ava was a demanding lover and wasted no time positioning Leland between her legs. If Leland had felt any doubts about Ava's desire for her, those doubts evaporated as Ava clung to her making whispered demands into her ear.

Ava lifted her hips upward against Leland's hand.

"More, I want to feel you inside," Ava directed Leland, her tone urgent.

Leland slid two fingers into Ava and began to thrust. "Oh, Ava."

Ava shifted under Leland so that her thigh was between Leland's legs. "Come with me." Ava's fingers teased at her entrance and Leland inhaled sharply as Ava pushed inside.

"I'm so close. Come with me, Leland. I want you…harder… yes! Come with me. Come with—"

Leland felt the orgasm rise like a flame, hot within her core, threatening to burst through her flesh and consume them both with searing intensity. Her breath quickened as they thrust together in an erotic dance until Ava cried out and dug her nails into Leland's back. Two more quick thrusts and Leland followed her over the edge into throbbing oblivion.

They clung to each other until Leland's heart rate slowed to near normal. Ava brushed damp hair away from Leland's forehead and pressed her lips there.

"I found our aircraft today." Ava spoke softly, moving her fingers up and down Leland's back. Leland lay partially on top of Ava, her head resting on Ava's chest.

"You did?"

"I'm going to figure out a way to get us to that plane, Leland. I'm going to get us out of here."

"Don't take any chances, Ava." Leland rose up on one elbow to look at her. "I believe that Maxine will help us get back to CCSF. She wants to come with us, and I want to help her return."

Ava held Leland's face in her hands. "You're a good person, Leland."

"So are you, Ava."

"Not like you. We're not the same in that way."

"I don't think you see yourself the way I do." Leland smiled at Ava, leaned down, and kissed her.

"I'm flattered that you think so highly of me, and I'm not convinced that it isn't the sex skewing your view." Ava playfully kissed her back. "But what I mean is that I believe you feel some larger purpose tugging at you. And you're the sort of selfless person who would heed that call. I'm not sure I would do that. I like my life the way it is. I like to be in control of my own life, and I like to keep it as uncomplicated as possible."

Leland wondered if that was a warning of sorts. She wondered if Ava was including the idea of a relationship as a complication. All Leland had ever known was complication. Being a member of the ruling elite was fraught with obligation. Ironically, these two days in captivity had been a small taste of freedom.

Ava tried to relax next to Leland. She had professed having feelings for Leland, and now she felt the familiar tug of panic as the implications of her words built scenarios inside her head. Yes, Leland was amazing, but she didn't really want a relationship. Or did she? Is this what was missing in her life? Someone who mattered, someone who understood her, or tried to?

Maybe if they talked more she could refocus her thoughts away from her fear of being trapped. Why did she equate love with the feeling of being trapped? It wasn't as if Leland seemed like the sort of person who would try to control her. But Leland's position in the world would require compromise on Ava's part if she were going to participate in that world. Was she ready to put her own life on hold for someone else?

"It's almost as if I can feel tension coming off your body into mine. What are you thinking about so intently?" Leland leaned up on one elbow. Her arm was still draped across Ava's body.

"Nothing."

"You can talk to me about it."

"Why is it when I tell you 'nothing' you never believe me?" Ava turned to face Leland.

"Call it a hunch." Leland smoothed her hand across Ava's stomach.

Ava wanted to change the subject. She didn't want to delve into the inner workings of her psyche with Leland. "Maxine said something odd to me earlier today. She said something about how I'd already contributed to real change in the cloud cities, but that I just don't know it yet."

Leland rolled onto her back, looking at the ceiling.

"Do you know what she's talking about?" Ava rolled on her side to face Leland.

"She believes that when you brought Cole to Easton from the ground you introduced pathogens into the urban environments that had previously not existed there."

"Meaning what?"

"The flu virus we've been tracking…well, she thinks Cole could have been a carrier."

Ava sat up beside Leland. "Well, so could Meredith. I found out today that she travels back and forth between the ground and the cloud cities regularly."

"Wait, what?"

"I found out from Faith that Meredith accesses the cities through the engineering decks. She flies back and forth from the ground to the cloud cities. I'm sure she's not using any sterilization or quarantine protocols. And Quinn isn't the only pilot here in the compound."

Leland was quiet as if she needed a minute to allow this to sink in.

"When were you going to tell me you suspected that Cole was a carrier for this flu?" She was trying not to get angry but failing.

"I wasn't keeping anything from you. I was going to talk to you about it. And it's not that you did anything wrong, Ava. You acted out of compassion for your friend, and this virus may have been a byproduct. And anyway, the virus itself isn't likely to turn into a pandemic, given its rate of transmission, but it does support my larger theory that the immune systems of the urban populations are compromised."

"Explain." Ava was trying not to sound as agitated as she felt. All she'd wanted was to get back to the city, get back to her life, and now Leland was telling her that people in the cities were unwell and possibly part of that was her fault. It wasn't as if she'd landed in the mountains intentionally. She'd had to make an emergency landing. Planes crashed sometimes. On the rare occasion when they did, there were rescue and quarantine procedures, and Ava hadn't used any of them. She'd thought Cole was going to die, and in fact, she almost did. She wasn't going to delay getting her to surgery by having her languish in a sterilization tube before being admitted.

"The synthesized food isn't giving us what we need. Separating from the Earth has weakened us as a population."

"And you knew this for how long?"

"I've been gathering data for a few months—"

"When were you going to say something?" Ava got out of bed and pulled on her pants and then her shirt. "Oh wait, didn't Maxine ask you about taking something…how did she say that?"

"I've been supplementing my diet with certain herbs to boost my immune system."

"And sharing this 'cure' with no one."

"It's not like that. As a scientist I can't just throw out a theory until I have the data to back it up. I was testing some herbal remedies on myself, but that certainly isn't scientifically sanctioned behavior. I had to be very sure my data was accurate because it would cost the companies that manufacture the synthetic food a lot of money to change their processes. It might even give rise to a new competing industry of natural food supplements, which might ultimately not solve the larger problem. I had to have convincing evidence."

Leland pulled the covering around her and sat on the edge of the bed. She tried to reach for Ava. "Why are you getting so angry?"

"I'm angry at myself. So fucking typical. The ruling elite care only that the companies they own might lose money. I can't believe that I thought you were different, but you're all the same."

"Ava, I do care. I care about you…I want to make things better for everyone. That's why I agree with what Maxine is proposing. All of these factors point toward a need for drastic change. I'm not going to go back and just let things keep moving forward as they are—"

Leland reached for Ava again and she pulled away. "Don't touch me."

"Ava." She could hear the hurt in Leland's voice, but she willed herself not to care.

"I need to be alone. I need to think. Please don't be here in my room when I get back." She closed the door behind her and stepped into the quiet darkness of the corridor. She turned left and started walking toward the outer exit.

Ava walked all the way to the main door before she realized it had been closed. She'd expected it to be open like it had been that night after the dust storm. She sank to the ground with her back to the door and gave in to her tears. These were angry tears. It only made her angrier that she was crying. She punched her thigh with her fist to distract herself from the aching in her chest.

Dirt seeped in around the edges of the heavy iron door and the lights along the corridor dimmed. She sat in the semi-darkness lecturing herself. She'd let her guard down with Leland, but obviously Leland had been holding back information from her.

As if she were some child who couldn't understand the whole truth of their situation. That infuriated her.

God, the elite were so removed from them all, above them all. Meredith, even in her supreme creepiness, was right about some things. The rich cared only about the rich, and ultimately their only goal was the acquisition of more wealth. It wasn't that her family wasn't well off. They were considered upper class, although not wealthy enough to be part of the truly elite. But it had always been clear to Ava that rising in society had been her mother's goal and her plan for Ava also. She'd seen her mother's prejudice come to the surface in all its ugliness when she'd brought Cole back to Easton for medical care.

And now she'd gone and fallen for the chancellor's daughter. Leland would inherit the wealth and position of her father. And even now she acted as if she were above everyone, deciding what was best for them as if they were children. Ava hated more than anything the feeling that someone else had any control over her life, and at this moment Leland did. She'd made love to Leland. She truly cared about Leland. She'd allowed Leland to make her miserable.

She rested her forehead on her arms across her knees and tried to take deep breaths. Ava tried to calm down, but now she felt trapped not only emotionally but physically. She needed to get the aircraft and get the hell out of here.

CHAPTER THIRTY-ONE

Leland dressed and went to her quarters. She felt as if she were walking through a dreamscape. What had just happened? She didn't understand why Ava had gotten so angry. It was as if Ava couldn't even look at her. Ava's entire body seemed to vibrate with rage as she'd pulled the door closed behind her.

Nausea overtook Leland, and she rushed to the small bathroom area to throw up. She splashed water on her face and tried to get her stomach to settle.

Should she give Ava time to calm down and then try to talk to her? She'd never had someone shut her out so completely so quickly and was at a loss of what to do to remedy the situation. They'd made love. Ava definitely had feelings for her. She'd said so. And then, as quickly as throwing a switch, the energy between them had shifted. It seemed that Ava couldn't get away from her fast enough, when all Leland wanted was for them to be close.

She was regretting that she hadn't told Ava everything when she'd asked. Ava had told Leland that she needed to know what Leland knew and still she'd held back. Why? Was she protecting Ava? Certainly Ava didn't need her protection. Self-loathing washed over Leland as she imagined herself as the patronizing elitist she must have appeared to be to Ava just now.

Was that who she really was? Did she really believe that the average citizen wasn't capable of handling the full truth? Maybe.

Was she kidding herself to believe she could lead some sort of societal transformation? Did she really have what it would take to make something like that happen?

Leland stood in front of one of the small windows that opened out onto the darkness. If the window had been large enough, she'd have considered climbing out of it into the desert so that she could just walk into the nothingness and disappear.

The world would not cease its spinning in her absence. Life could continue on its current trajectory, happily oblivious to its looming demise. Maybe that would be a better course than facing the bitter medicine required to correct its course.

Chapter Thirty-two

Ava slowly fought through a haze of sleep. She thought she'd been dreaming, but now she realized the sound she'd heard was real. The unmistakable sound of an aircraft engine, and it sounded as if it was close by. She splashed water on her face and rushed for the door. She'd slept in her clothes, and they looked like it.

She pushed through a small group of people as she made her way quickly down the corridor back to the exit tunnel that had been closed the previous night. It was very early, but still the sun was intensely bright. There was no humidity in the air to dampen or defuse its light.

Ava exited the large opening just in time to see two individuals leave Quinn alone near the cargo door of her aircraft. There were boxes near the loading ramp stacked haphazardly around as if waiting to be packed. But Quinn was alone, and she hadn't noticed Ava when she turned and receded back into the darkened cargo bay.

Ava made tracks to follow her. She stormed up the loading ramp and into the main cargo area. It took a few seconds for her eyes to adjust to the lower light of the interior space.

"Quinn!"

"Hey there, Cap. You shouldn't be in here. I'm prepping the ship for departure." Quinn seemed completely nonchalant and unthreatened by Ava's presence. Maybe she was just trying to piss Ava off by her indifference. It was working.

Ava was still angry from the previous night's fight with Leland, and she'd like nothing better than to be able to take it out on Quinn.

"If this craft is departing then I plan to be on it." Ava took a few steps closer to Quinn. It was too late by the time she noticed Quinn had a firearm holstered at her hip. She pulled it, halting Ava's advance.

"That'd be fine by me, Cap. Everyone's gonna think you flew this bird anyway, so you might as well be on it."

Ava looked around her for the first time, and her stomach knotted with the realization of what she was seeing. It looked like a bomb, bulbous at one end, tapering toward what looked like fins at the other end. It was enormous, and it was strapped down and anchored in the center of the cargo hold.

"You're going to discharge a weapon near that?"

"Oh, you noticed our little vintage explosive device? Explosives are so volatile. Maybe I should put this away. Something about seeing you brings out the worst in me." Quinn slowly holstered the pulse weapon.

"Where the hell did you get this?"

"Did you ever hear of the Nevada Proving Grounds? We're only about sixty miles from where they used to set these things off just to see how much damage they could do."

Ava stood in stunned silence.

"The ruling elite have always been assholes. There's some comfort in knowing things never really change. They test their bombs, they wage wars, they hoard fuel and wealth, and the rest of us…well, we suffer for it don't we?"

Ava took a few steps back toward the cargo opening, and Quinn followed her.

"What? Did you change your mind about getting on this flight?" Quinn stepped out the wide cargo bay door and picked up a tablet and began to type.

"What's going on?" Ava followed Quinn, but kept a safe distance.

"Your aircraft is going to make a one-way flight to CC Easton. Unfortunately, the landing gear will fail and the bird will crash in a fireball." Quinn looked up from the tablet and smiled.

"You're crazy. Why would you do that? What is that going to solve?"

"Well, it seems that there's a trade summit in Easton right now, and everyone who's anyone is there. We thought we'd crash the party, literally."

"I'm not going to let you do this."

"Oh, yeah, is that right, Cap? What are you gonna do about it?" Quinn put the tablet into a bag slung over her shoulder and took a step toward Ava.

"I'm gonna start by kicking your ass, Quinn." Ava didn't flinch when Quinn advanced on her. She held her ground, and when Quinn took the first swing, she ducked, quickly coming back at her with a strong right to her jaw.

Quinn staggered back a step then lunged at Ava, grabbing her and landing several quick blows to her ribs before Ava could break away. They started circling each other, creating small dust clouds around their feet. Ava wanted to get the pulse weapon, and she was trying to decide the best way to do just that when Quinn pulled the weapon and aimed it right at her chest.

Beck scanned the area. "There!"

"Where?" Jenna tried to follow Beck's gaze.

"By the aircraft. I've got visual on Ava." She pointed toward the cargo bay door. She and Jenna had approached the compound at first light and had stationed themselves behind a partially crumbling rock outcropping waiting for some movement around the aircraft.

The craft had set down just minutes earlier, and it didn't take long for Ava to show up. They couldn't hear anything from where they were hiding, but the body language between Quinn and Ava seemed to indicate that they were arguing. That was confirmed when they began to exchange blows. There was clearly something going on, then Quinn pulled a pulse weapon and aimed it at Ava, who was unarmed.

"I'm not going to sit here and let her shoot Ava." Jenna pulled her rifle and sighted it on Quinn.

"Don't kill Quinn. We need her for questioning."

"I won't kill her." Jenna squeezed the trigger, and the pulse round discharge pierced the silent arid desert air.

Quinn recoiled as she was struck in the shoulder. She spun in Jenna's direction and fired. The shot missed their position but sent them for cover as debris rained down around them from the fragmented rock they were hiding behind.

They saw Ava scramble for cover away from Quinn's position behind a large cargo crate.

"We need to find Leland before this escalates. Because now they definitely know we're here." Beck was scanning the opening to the tunnel that seemed to lead into the compound below ground. "If you cover me I can make a run for the entrance over there."

"I don't like it. You'd be on your own. We'd both be on our own."

"I'm not sure we have a choice." Beck tried to rise for a better look at the tunnel entrance when another pulse round struck nearby. "Shit!"

"We need to get closer if we're going to disarm Quinn."

"That wasn't Quinn. We've got a second shooter. I think it's Meredith." Beck tried to angle for a better view as another round made impact near her head.

"Cover me. I'm going to move toward those rocks there." Jenna motioned with her head to another rock formation between where they were now and the aircraft. A random assortment of cargo crates that was stacked between Quinn and Meredith's position and the rocks would offer her some cover for her movements.

Beck nodded. "Okay, wait until my first shot, then go. You cover me and I'll follow."

Beck fired twice. One shot shattered a cargo crate sending its shredded contents in every direction, which offered enough of a distraction for Jenna to scurry for cover. Jenna immediately took a firing stance and Beck moved closer.

CHAPTER THIRTY-THREE

The sound of a weapon firing jolted Leland from sleep. She couldn't believe she'd fallen asleep at all, but she must have at some point, and now her heart was thumping so hard in her chest that it threatened to pound through her skin. Who was shooting? Her first salient thought was of Ava. Where was she? Was she safe?

She dressed quickly and stumbled into the hallway only to be caught by two of the people who'd been with Meredith the first night of their capture.

Leland struggled against her two captors, but she couldn't break free. She desperately wanted to find Ava. She fought them as they began to drag her along the corridor away from the main entrance. This wasn't what she'd thought would happen. She believed Maxine when she said they would leave together. Maybe Ava was right. Maybe she was naïve.

"Where are you taking me?" Leland tried again to slow their forward motion.

Leland heard another pulse round echo through the stone tunnel. The sound made her two captors stop and look back in the direction they'd just come. Leland turned also, and her heart rate increased when she caught sight of Maxine and Faith heading toward them.

"Release her!" Maxine shouted as she approached.

"We're taking her to the second aircraft. Meredith's orders." The man was still holding Leland's arm, but his tone with Maxine was respectful rather than defiant.

Another shot reverberated along the rock walls surrounding them. The two holding Leland clearly seemed nervous.

"I will take Leland. You go find Meredith. Does anyone but me hear shots being fired?" asked Maxine.

They reluctantly released Leland. Meredith's underlings brushed past Maxine and began to run toward the main exit corridor. Leland, Maxine, and Faith walked back toward her room.

"Maxine, what's going on?" Leland wanted some answers.

"Something terrible I fear. We must get you out of here."

They passed the door to Leland's quarters without stopping and instead headed toward the exit tunnel themselves. They crested the opening just as another shot was fired, and Leland got her first glimpse of Ava crouched behind a cargo crate. Quinn and Meredith were several feet away firing away from the compound. Then she saw a flash and realized that others were firing back. Ava seemed to be trying to edge closer to those who were firing on Quinn. Did she know them? Leland wanted to call out to Ava, but at the same time she didn't want to reveal Ava's position.

"Faith, there's a pulse weapon in the study. Get it. Quickly!" Maxine pushed Leland against the wall, out of view and out of harm's way.

What was going on? Leland leaned out and quickly looked about. She felt Maxine's hand on her arm pulling her back to safer cover.

❖

"There! I have eyes on Leland." Beck motioned with her hand toward the main entrance. She yelled in Leland's direction. "Leland! Stay back! We'll come to you!"

Jenna stood up and fired in rapid succession. As the last round blew up another cargo crate, Ava scuttled into position behind the rock with them.

"Jenna! I can't believe you're here!" Ava and Jenna embraced briefly.

"Believe it."

"Things are worse than you think." Ava sank back against the rock, her face smeared with red dirt.

"Really? Because they seem pretty bad." Jenna motioned in Beck's direction. "Ava, this is Beck. She's with the Bureau, and she's here to get you and Leland out."

"What do you mean things are worse than we think?" Beck needed an understanding of the situation quickly. Jenna seemed certain of Ava's innocence, but Beck was still unsure.

The engines of the aircraft came to life causing Beck to stiffen. If they thought they were going to take Leland with them they would have to do it over her dead body.

"We can't let that plane leave." Ava's tone was urgent. "There's a bomb on that aircraft, and it's headed for Easton."

"What?" Beck and Jenna asked in unison.

"They're going to remotely lift off and then the autopilot is set to take it the rest of the way. But they've disabled the landing gear. It'll crash when it reaches CC Easton."

Beck crouched next to the wall, her mind raced through possible options, but as she strategized a plan of attack, the engines reached a higher pitch, indicating they were almost at full power.

"I need to get on that plane." Ava's voice was calm but loud enough to be heard over the engines.

"No." Jenna was quick to respond.

"I'm the only one who can do this. I'm sure Quinn didn't change the pilot access codes. That's my plane. I can log in and override the autopilot. It's the only way." Ava leaned out just a little to check the status of the aircraft. "The cargo door is still open. If you cover me, I can make a run for it. But it's gotta be right now."

"Ava, it's too dangerous. What if Quinn did change the codes?" Jenna put her hand on Ava's arm.

"Trust me, she's not that smart. Listen, I can do this. Everyone we care about is in Easton...Sophie, Sarah, my mom...I can do this, Jenna."

"This might work." Beck didn't have a plan that seemed better, not since that plan needed to happen in the next sixty seconds or so. Time was running out as the plane powered up. "Ava, you're sure?"

"I'm sure." She nodded at Beck, her gaze focused and fierce.

"Okay, wait until we lay down cover fire."

Jenna and Beck began to alternate fire, pinning both Quinn and Meredith down behind some shipping crates. Ava dashed for the cargo bay door just as it was beginning to close as the craft slowly began to rise. If they'd waited thirty more seconds they'd have run out of time. Beck got a glimpse of Ava as she tumbled over the edge of the door seconds before it closed. The plane lifted off in a cloud of dust and headed east.

"You were right about Ava. She's a goddamn hero." Beck was happy to be wrong in this case. She hoped Ava really could pull this off.

CHAPTER THIRTY-FOUR

A va tumbled down the slanted surface of the cargo bay door as the seal closed. The bay's interior was darkened, with only emergency low wattage lighting active. She got to her feet and hit the round primary light sensor with her open palm. Lights flickered to life in the cargo area and farther along into the passenger compartment. She hustled past the bomb toward the cockpit hoping desperately that she was right about Quinn not thinking to reset the pilot security ID codes in the onboard computer.

She dropped into the pilot's seat and punched her personal code on the keyboard. *Please work, please work, please work.*

The computer interface was active, awaiting input. She was in! She checked her location in the navigation system. She needed a dead zone on the map. Ava didn't want this bomb impacting CC Easton, but she also didn't want it to destroy any communities on the ground. She needed to bring the aircraft down in the desert.

While she was still searching for suitable coordinates, she banked the craft slightly north. Ironically, she was heading back to the old testing grounds north of Vegas that Quinn had mentioned earlier. That seemed like the most fitting landing site for this device of resurrected devastation.

Ava entered new coordinates and initiated the aircraft's descent, then reengaged the autopilot function. She took another minute to try to reroute and reconnect the landing gear functions, but she couldn't bring them back online, and she was running out of time.

She leapt from the pilot's chair, ran through the passenger compartment, and moved quickly toward the back of the plane. In the cargo area she dug in the storage lockers along the wall for a parachute. Within seconds, she was wearing the chute apparatus. She punched the safety release in the large open bay. The enormous steel cargo door slowly opened to reveal the vast desert beneath. Small untethered items within the cargo area swept past her and out the opening. A cargo net, paper cups, a cushion, and several sheets of loose paper were all sucked swiftly past her into the open air. The tilt of the floor beneath her increased as the plane entered into its final descent.

Ava backed toward the door and was caught up as debris herself in the suction of the plane roaring through the arid sky. As soon as she was clear of the backdraft of the craft, Ava pulled the ripcord on the chute. Her body was instantly jerked up and away from the flight path. She watched the plane move swiftly away from her as she was pulled in the opposite direction.

Minutes later, Ava made bone-jarring contact with the barren earth. She'd tried to come down in a controlled tumble to save her legs from completely absorbing the shock of her landing, but she'd failed. The wind at surface level was too strong, and a sudden gust yanked her backward a split second before she was able to regain her footing. The still open chute dragged Ava several yards on her back.

As she fought to release the chute, Ava felt a heaviness in her chest she'd never known. Her heart, previously impervious, ached for Leland. What had her last words to Leland been? As she struggled to free herself, she couldn't remember. All she could recall was that she hadn't said what she'd felt. She hadn't said what mattered. Ava frantically worked at the release clasp for the straps across her chest as the chute continued to drag her across rough sandstone. Ava glanced sideways and saw the rock approaching fast, but she was unable to alter her body's trajectory. Her head made impact and blackness filled her senses.

CHAPTER THIRTY-FIVE

Leland saw Ava scramble onto the aircraft as it left the ground in a flurry of pulse blasts. She couldn't believe what she'd seen. Why had Ava made a run for the plane? Who was firing on Meredith and Quinn? She felt Maxine tug her back into the cover of the exit tunnel.

Mere minutes after the aircraft left their location, an enormous burst of light, followed seconds later by shock waves of a sounding blast rippled over her. Leland felt the vibration of the blast in her chest. She staggered back a step in shock. Her mind couldn't quite process the sequence of events she'd just witnessed.

Leland obviously hadn't been the only one who'd been shocked by the explosion on the horizon to the north. Meredith stood and looked in the direction of the detonation, openly revealing her position. A shot was fired, and Meredith pitched backward onto the ground. Quinn stood and fired in the direction of the shot and was also taken down by a subsequent pulse round.

Leland watched as two women quickly advanced on Quinn's position. One of the women kicked Quinn's weapon away from her; the other bent to check Meredith who hadn't moved since she'd hit the ground.

Slowly, as if her muscles were heavy and sluggish, Leland stepped from the exit into the open air. Maxine hurried past her and knelt beside her sister. The dark-haired woman kept her gun on Quinn; the other woman walked toward Leland.

"Leland Argosy, I'm Rebecca Scott with the Federal Bureau of Security."

Leland looked at Beck but didn't speak. She blinked several times trying to grasp the details of what had just happened. "Was that the plane? The blast? Was that blast from the aircraft Ava just boarded?" Leland felt confused, like a child. She needed someone to explain to her what had just happened.

"Leland, are you hurt?" Beck holstered her weapon and put her hands on Leland's arms.

"Was that Ava's plane?" Leland asked again.

"Yes."

The one-word confirmation made Leland dizzy. She bent over, bracing her hands on her knees, gasping for air.

Beck tried to understand the reaction Leland was having. She seemed as if she was in shock. Beck placed a hand on Leland's back in an attempt to comfort her in some way. She was clearly in distress.

"Beck?"

Beck looked up to see Faith standing a few feet away holding a pulse weapon at her side. She looked as if she'd just seen a ghost. Beck flinched, and Faith seemed to realize she was still holding the gun. She dropped it near her feet and stood silently as if she was waiting to see what Beck's response would be.

Beck's next action was based solely on instinct. She stepped quickly to Faith and pulled her into an embrace. "Faith, thank God you're safe." Beck felt Faith lean into her and return the embrace. Beck wanted nothing more than to pull Faith off to the side of all of the mayhem and reconnect. There were so many questions and so many unfinished arguments between them. But this wasn't the time for any of it.

"Beck, why are you here?" Faith pulled away and looked at her face.

"I'm here to rescue Leland." Beck moved back to Leland who still seemed unstable on her feet. "Leland, why don't you sit for a minute?" Beck guided her to one of the still intact cargo crates.

"Can you just stay with her for a moment?" Beck asked. Faith nodded and Beck went to check in with Jenna.

Quinn was injured and writhing around on the ground at Jenna's feet. She'd put restraints on Quinn's wrists but had left her unsympathetically lying in the dirt. Blood from her shoulder and upper arm stained her shirt.

"How's Leland?" Jenna asked.

"In shock. Meredith?"

"Deceased."

Beck stood looking down at Meredith's prone figure. A woman who looked remarkably similar to Meredith knelt beside her body. She reached to close Meredith's open and unfocused eyes. Then she looked up at Beck, the wet paths of tears glistening on her cheeks.

"Meredith was my sister," she said, as if anticipating Beck's question. The woman stood and looked down at her sister once more before introducing herself. "I am Dr. Maxine Ray."

"Rebecca Scott. I'm sorry for the loss of your sister."

"I lost my sister a long, long time ago, Ms. Scott."

"I need to go look for Ava. We need to go look for Ava." Leland was walking toward them.

"I agree." Jenna holstered her weapon. "There's a good chance, a very good chance, that Ava got off that plane before it went down."

"We need to get Leland back to CC Easton now. Right now. It may already be too late." Beck wanted to find Ava too, but her priority was getting Leland back to her father while he was still alive. She didn't think they had a minute to spare if she was going to make that happen.

"I'm not going anywhere until I know Ava is safe." Leland had a determined look on her face.

"I feel the same way. I'm not going to leave Ava on foot, in the desert," said Jenna.

"Leland, this is Jenna Bookman, our pilot. Who I'm sorry to say can't stay behind if we're going to get you back to CC Easton as quickly as is necessary." Jenna started to say something else, but Beck raised a hand to stop her. "I understand your concerns, you know I do, but you signed on for this detail, Jenna, and that means your first priority is getting Leland back to the city."

"Why such a sense of urgency?" asked Leland.

Beck didn't want to have to tell Leland of her father's condition in the midst of all this chaos, but she needed for Leland to understand the gravity of the situation. "Leland, your father is extremely ill. We need to get you back to Easton immediately."

"My father?" Leland looked as if she was trying to synthesize this new bit of information. "Even still, I can't leave. I won't leave without knowing—"

"I'll go for Ava." Faith touched Leland's arm as she spoke.

Leland turned toward Faith.

"I'll find her and I'll send word as soon as I have her." Faith sounded confident.

"Thank you, Faith," said Jenna.

"I'll go with her." Maxine had joined the discussion late, but her commitment to find Ava seemed as resolute as Faith's.

"Listen, as far as I'm concerned, everyone in this compound is under suspicion, and I plan to question the entire settlement when I return." No one was off the hook here, and Beck wanted to make sure that was clear.

"Beck, I know you have your orders and you have protocols you must follow, but things here are not as black-and-white as you may imagine." Leland's gaze was so fierce that Beck took a step back.

"I'm sorry if my orders sounded callous. My primary concern, Ms. Argosy, is getting you safely back to CC Easton as quickly as possible. Your father needs you."

Beck watched a series of emotions play out across Leland's face. After a moment, with great reluctance Leland agreed to leave with Beck and Jenna. They would use their ATV to return to their small aircraft. Faith and Maxine would drive in a solar-powered rover toward the smoke plume still visible on the horizon. Faith would message Beck with any update about Ava.

Maxine asked several in the crowd that had gathered around them from the compound to move Quinn to a secure location until Beck could return for her. She also asked that Meredith be moved to the infirmary.

"Please find her." Leland made an earnest plea directly to Faith.

"Go to your father, Leland. I will find Ava. I promise."

Beck hustled Leland toward their ATV. She hoped they would make it back to Easton before it was too late. Either way, Leland was safe and in custody. She held out small hope that Ava had survived.

Chapter Thirty-six

L eland sat in silence looking out the window of the small military transport as it winged its way toward CC Easton. Her heart had been heavy with fatigue and worry as she climbed into the small aircraft leaving Ava behind. How had things gone so horribly wrong so quickly?

They'd been making love, then they'd argued, and Leland had never gotten the opportunity to explain her actions to Ava. And now, now her father lay dying and she was going to face whatever situation awaited her at his bedside, alone. Like never before, Leland wished for a sibling to share the looming burden of her father's passing. But she had no siblings.

The four-hour flight to Easton seemed to take only minutes as Leland's mind reeled with all that had happened in the last twenty-four hours. She heard muffled voices from the cockpit as Jenna communicated with the flight tower about their approach. Beck had been seated in the copilot's seat, but as Leland sensed the aircraft banking for its approach to CC Easton, Beck took the seat next to her in the small, six-seat passenger compartment.

"We'll be landing soon."

Leland nodded. Tears would have been appropriate, but at the moment, she felt numb. Now was not the time for tears anyway. Now was the time for strength.

"Listen, I know Faith. She'll find Ava. You can count on it. And as soon as she does, she'll get a message to me. I gave her my secure line." Beck's posture was a bit stiff. She seemed to be attempting to be comforting but respectfully distant at the same time.

Leland nodded again. "Thank you." Her voice broke and she cleared her throat. The cabin darkened as they passed through the landing tube, signaling they were almost on the tarmac in Easton.

"We should get you into the sterilization tube since you've been on the ground. Actually, the tube on this craft seats four so we can all get in at the same time." There were rare instances when people had to be quarantined or go through the UV sterilization protocol before reentry. But Leland knew it no longer mattered.

"Contamination has already happened. Contamination will be what saves us." Leland put her hand on Beck's arm. "But please keep this confidential for now."

Beck nodded, but Leland could see the unasked questions in her eyes.

They disembarked. A small crowd of very serious looking, dark clad individuals from the Security Bureau surrounded them as they exited the plane. Beck shouted orders, and the small sea of dark suits separated to reveal a waiting maglev transport.

Jenna held the door for Beck and Leland who climbed into the transport first. Beck explained to Leland that the Bureau would most definitely request a debriefing with Leland, but that would have to wait.

The brief ride to the medical lab was a blur of urban concrete and glass. Cool and gray in contrast to the arid, red warmth of the desert. Leland hardly knew Beck, but in the last four hours she'd become Leland's lifeline. She feared she was becoming unmoored, and Beck's solidness was the only force keeping her tethered to her own body.

She studied Beck while Beck was speaking softly but firmly to someone over her comm unit. She was focused and beautifully strong. When Leland faced forward, she saw that Jenna had been watching her. As soon as she'd turned, Jenna quickly averted her eyes. Leland suspected that Jenna was as worried about Ava as she was. She'd gathered from the brief discussion on the ground that Jenna and Ava had some history together, in what capacity she wasn't sure. Maybe they'd flown together.

The transport pulled up next to the med lab's rear exit. As they approached her father's room, Leland could see that a crowd was gathered in the hallway. She didn't want to speak with anyone and said as much to Beck.

"Just stay close to me. No one will bother you." Beck put a protective arm around Leland's waist. She could hear snippets of conversation in hushed tones as Beck and Jenna ushered her through those gathered until they were at the door to her father's room. Richard, her father's personal assistant, was in the room. And his mistress, Estelle, hovered near his bedside. Estelle was tastefully dressed for a change in a black skirt and sweater. She looked as if she'd been crying.

Leland moved to the side of her father's bed. He looked deathly pale. She could hear the rasping of his labored breathing above the hum of the machines near his bed.

So this was it? This was how death claimed us. No amount of wealth or status could spare us the frail and failing human condition.

"Will all of you please leave the room?" Leland's request was soft but firm.

Beck began to usher the others out the door. Richard touched Leland's arm as he stepped past her.

Before she followed the others, Beck turned back. "I'll be right outside the door if you need me, Leland."

Leland nodded. "Thank you, Beck."

She pulled a chair close to the bedside and lifted her father's hand in hers. She leaned forward, pressing her lips against his cool skin. His hand was heavy and unresponsive in hers.

All the things they'd left unsaid began to fill the airspace around them. And those things would never be said unless she said them now. Would he hear her? Was he still even in the room with her? His body seemed so changed as to be unrecognizable to her, his once strong facial features sunken and sallow.

"Father." Leland's voice cracked, and she wiped at a tear that trailed slowly down her cheek. "Oh, Father." She could hold back no longer and began to sob. She buried her face into the sheets near where she still held his unresponsive hand.

It wasn't as if she and her father had been close. It wasn't as if they even fully understood each other. But still, this was a connection she hadn't wanted to lose. She wasn't ready to be without him.

And there were the unanswered questions. Did he have regrets about his life? Was he afraid of death? Did he love her? As she reflected back, she realized he rarely used the word love, even when talking about things he cherished.

She should have made more of an effort to know him.

What did any of it matter now? She'd lost Ava. She'd lost her family. She was adrift. They'd made it to the hospital before her father had technically died, but she sensed he was no longer with her, even as the rhythmic blip of the cardiac machine begged to differ with her assessment.

Leland leaned over and pressed her lips to his forehead. She stood looking down at him for another few minutes when it dawned on her that the cardiac machine had grown silent. A slight hum remained, but the digital line that had previously indicated a slightly irregular, weak pulse was now flat.

Her father had slipped away while she'd studied his face and she hadn't seen it. Had there been a presence besides hers in the room that now seemed missing? No. His life force had receded without flourish or fanfare. There had been no sign at all of its passing.

Leland had expected to feel something, to have some obvious sense of his passing, but in the instant of his death there had been only stillness, nothingness. In the end of it all, we are not in control. We are transient and vulnerable.

She heard the door open behind her. A doctor walked to the other side of the bed; no doubt he'd seen from the nurses' station that the chancellor's heart had stopped. She watched him mark time of death on a small tablet he replaced in the pocket of his white coat.

Beck had followed the doctor into the room and now guided Leland to a chair. She collapsed into it then leaned forward, resting her face in her hands.

After a moment, she looked up at Beck. "My father is dead."

CHAPTER THIRTY-SEVEN

Ava's first foggy sensation was thirst. Quickly followed by the sensation of something tugging at her chest. Her eyes fluttered open, and she saw a silhouetted figure of a woman looming over her. She panicked as the last minutes of her ordeal flashed back to her dizzy brain in a frenzied slide show. She frantically tried to ward off whoever was leaning over her.

"Ava, it's me, Faith! Stop fighting me. You're going to be okay."

"What? Faith?"

Another shadow joined the first. The sun was too bright. Her eyes hurt, her head hurt, her body ached, and she was incredibly thirsty.

"I need to unclip this parachute. It has you pinned to the rock."

Ava closed her eyes and tried to will herself to relax. She was alive.

"This isn't working. Hold still. I'm going to cut the straps." Faith pulled a knife from her belt, and within seconds, Ava felt the tension tugging against her body release as the chute was swept farther into the desert by the wind.

"Can you sit up?" Maxine asked. "I have some water."

Even in her weakened state, the sight of Maxine made Ava recoil. She tried to get to her feet, but her balance was off, her legs weak, so all she could manage was to scuttle back a couple of feet.

"Ava, we're not here to hurt you." Maxine's tone was calm, soothing, but Ava still wasn't convinced.

"Where's Meredith?" Ava's voice cracked from thirst.

"Please, drink some water. You're dehydrated." Maxine extended the canteen in her direction. Ava accepted the water and drank.

The first attempts at swallowing were followed by fits of coughing, but eventually, Ava was able to get some water down her parched throat.

"Meredith is dead and Quinn is wounded," Faith answered. She'd been kneeling near Ava and sank back onto her heels.

"And Leland? Where's Leland?" When Ava climbed into the back of the aircraft, all hell was breaking loose around it, and she needed to know what had happened.

"Leland is fine, but she had to go to Easton because her father is very ill."

Leland was gone. She was gone and there was no way for Ava to reach her. Her heart sank. She needed to see Leland. She needed to apologize for all the awful things she'd said to her.

"Beck and Jenna flew Leland back to CC Easton. Her father is deathly ill. He's not expected to live." As Faith spoke, she seemed to be studying the side of Ava's face. She tentatively touched it with her fingertips. "We need to clean this head wound and get you out of the sun. Can you stand?"

Ava ignored Faith's question and instead asked one of her own. "Why are you here?" She was looking directly at Maxine. There was accusation in her voice, and she made no attempt to conceal it.

"Ava, I am not my sister. I know you don't trust me, but I am not your enemy. I didn't know about the bomb, and if I had I would have stopped her."

"She's telling the truth, Ava. We came for you because we care about you. There's no other agenda at work here. You can relax."

Ava nodded and made a feeble attempt to stand, but realized fairly quickly that she needed assistance from Faith to get to her feet. Her head swam and nausea caused her to bend over in an attempt to settle her stomach. As she looked down, she realized her hands and arms were smeared with dried blood from shallow cuts and scrapes she'd no doubt received from being dragged across the sandstone by the tangled chute.

"Are you okay to walk?" Faith knelt beside her, looking up at her face.

Ava nodded. "I just felt queasy. I'll be okay. Let's get out of here."

As they rode back to the compound, Ava reflected on all that had happened. She found it unbelievable that after the role Quinn had played in everything that Quinn had come through almost unscathed. Almost.

She wasn't sorry to hear of Meredith's death. She was sorry for Maxine. She knew that it must have been hard for Maxine. Regardless of the ideological distance that had developed between them, Meredith was still her sister.

Ava leaned back against the headrest in the rover. Dry wind whipped across her face from the open-air vehicle stinging her sunburned skin, but at least she was sheltered from the sun, and she hoped soon this ordeal would be over.

Then what?

Then she would find Leland and ask for her forgiveness.

CHAPTER THIRTY-EIGHT

L eland signed the paperwork at the morgue for her father's remains to be cremated. The service would take place in Paris.

In the first hours after she assumed the position of chancellor, Leland closed ranks, populating her personal staff with those individuals she trusted implicitly. That short list of names now included Beck Scott and Jenna Bookman. She was keeping Richard close also, as he had been her father's confidant and she trusted his assessment of recent events in the statehouse in CC Paris that she'd not been privy to.

There had apparently been some backroom jockeying for positions of power as her father's condition had deteriorated, and she'd not been on site to witness it so Richard's perspective would be valuable in the days and weeks that followed.

Leland had other cabinet positions to fill, but those could wait until after her father's service.

The viceroys who'd gathered in CC Easton for the trade summit reconvened to witness Leland being sworn in as chancellor. The ceremony had been somber in tone, given the circumstance of her ascension. Leland felt the weight of all eyes on her and all expectations on her shoulders as she exited the great hall to the sound of reserved applause.

As Beck and two other security personnel escorted Leland to a private aircraft waiting to take her to Paris, she had one thought about the viceroys. They had no idea of the storm that was coming.

Leland was playing nice. Deferring to seasoned members of the ruling elite on smaller matters that needed immediate attention. She didn't want to make any sudden moves that would tip her hand. She needed to gain their trust, at least in the short term. She wanted them to believe for now that she would maintain the direction of leadership her father had taken, that she would do her part to shore up the status quo, when in reality her deepest desire was to dismantle it.

From any external observation, Leland probably appeared to be a bastion of calm. But inside she was a sea of torment. Years of standing in her father's shadow, on public display, had schooled her in the art of hiding her true feelings. Those lessons were serving her well as she moved through the proceedings that had to be endured to bring her father's life to a close and usher her into the next phase of hers.

Two hours later, Jenna landed the small aircraft in CC Paris, and in another fifteen minutes, they were finally on the grounds of her father's estate, a multi-storied steel and concrete structure that featured terraced gardens at alternating corners.

Estelle, her father's mistress, had asked to accompany Leland back to Paris, but Leland had politely requested some time alone with her father's things. She wanted a chance to go through her father's effects with Richard before even the smallest detail had been disturbed. Having an opportunity to spend time in his quarters without disruption would be like getting a snapshot of his state of mind just before he became ill. But she wouldn't be able to do that right away, and in the short term she'd asked Beck to secure her father's quarters and keep everything under constant surveillance.

The space was deathly quiet when their small party arrived. Leland was exhausted. She'd barely slept the night before her departure from the desert, and worry over Ava hovered at the periphery of her thoughts. Where was she? Was she hurt? Was she even alive?

Leland's insides felt hollow. An incomparable emptiness where once she'd had feeling.

"Beck, could you accompany me to my quarters?"

"Certainly." As she stepped away from the other two security officers, Beck gave them quiet instruction. They nodded as she left them and stepped into the lift with Leland.

They rode in silence to one of the higher floors, to Leland's private rooms. Leland was grateful that Beck wasn't someone who felt the need to fill every empty space with conversation. Beck was comfortable with silence. This was becoming one of many of Beck's traits that Leland valued.

Once they were in Leland's private quarters, Beck stopped respectfully just inside the closed door. Leland started across the room but then turned and walked back a few steps so that she was standing very close to Beck, who seemed uncertain as to what was expected of her.

"Beck, I want to thank you…for everything." Leland's voice was thick with emotion. She was having a hard time talking around the lump in her throat.

"Leland, can I speak frankly?"

"Please do."

"You've been through an incredible ordeal, and it's not over yet. Why don't you sit and I'll have someone bring you some food?"

Leland nodded as tears slowly slipped down her cheekbones. Beck was right. She was exhausted.

Beck turned to reach for the door but hesitated. She took a step back, and in a huge breach of protocol, drew Leland into a tender hug. "Don't forget that you have friends here, Leland. Everything is going to be okay."

Beck was a few inches shorter than Leland. She pressed her cheek into Beck's hair and allowed herself to be held.

As they released each other, Beck's comm unit buzzed.

Beck read the message and Leland watched as her demeanor brightened. "It's from Faith. They've found Ava and she's alive." Relief flooded Leland's system and she swayed on her feet. Ava was alive. She repeated the words inside her head. *Ava was alive!*

"Faith says they found her within about six hours of our departure. They weren't able to radio until they returned to the compound. For some reason there was a delay in the delivery of this message so I just now got it. Faith says Ava is in good condition."

"Please tell Faith that I owe her a huge debt of gratitude."

"Jenna and I will make arrangements to return for Quinn and Ava tomorrow. We'll bring her back to Paris with us."

"I'd like to go with you."

"Ms. Argosy, I'd prefer that you not—"

"Beck, I don't want to see her here, not like this." Leland swept her hands in an arc. "This, this is all too much."

"Are you sure you're well enough to travel? You've also been through a lot."

"Beck, if I don't see Ava as soon as possible I guarantee I will not be well.

"I'll make the arrangements."

CHAPTER THIRTY-NINE

B eck watched Leland walk in the direction of Ava's quarters. Her first agenda item after returning to the desert compound was to check the room where Quinn was being held. Sentries had been posted to make sure she stayed put. The community's doctor had seen to Quinn's wounds to her shoulder and arm. She wouldn't be firing a pulse weapon any time soon, or piloting an aircraft. She'd be appearing in front of a judiciary board in Paris as soon as they all returned to the city.

Beck didn't have natural psychic abilities, but she saw a court-martial and jail time in Quinn's future. The thought of that bit of justice being served made her happy. And Jenna had taken out Meredith for good. The insurgency had been shattered.

Beck felt satisfied, proud even. She'd done her job. She'd found Leland and she'd aborted a terrorist attack on CC Easton. Actually, all the credit for that epic save had to go to Ava. What a surprise she'd turned out to be. And in this particular instance, Beck was happy to be surprised.

"What are you smiling about?"

Beck looked up to see Faith approaching her in the corridor. "Hi."

"Maxine told me that you were back on site to retrieve Quinn and Ava. I'd hoped we might have a few minutes to talk if you... well, if you'd like to do that."

Faith seemed unsure of herself, a highly unusual situation based on Beck's past experiences with her. The truth was they had a lot of history and also many years of living life apart. They both had good reason for trepidation about reconnecting, but Beck wanted nothing more than a few moments alone with Faith. Ever since the shooting, glimpses and memories of Faith had been crowding every free thought when her mind wasn't occupied with some task.

"I'd like a chance to talk to you also. I'm sorry I had to leave so abruptly. It was urgent that we get to CC Easton."

"How is Leland's father?"

"He passed away shortly after we made it back."

"I'm sorry to hear that. And I'm sorry for Leland."

Beck wasn't sure what to suggest. This wasn't her turf. They were in Faith's place.

"Is there somewhere we could go to talk?" asked Beck.

"We could go to my quarters. It's this way." Faith tilted her head in the direction she'd just come, and Beck fell into step beside her as they walked back up the long, dimly lit corridor.

Once they were inside Faith's small living space with the door closed, Beck was wrestling with the urge to kiss her. To hell with all the history, to hell with their youthful stubbornness, she now knew that the kind of chemistry she'd shared with Faith was a once in a lifetime event.

When she'd been young, Beck had foolishly believed that love would find her easily and often. She'd been wrong. It wasn't until she was older that she more fully understood the connection she'd had with Faith. At least she thought she did. She hoped she did. But she was having a hard time reading Faith's mood.

When they'd hugged briefly, Faith had returned the embrace, but that might have been nothing more than polite affection for an ex-girlfriend.

"Can I offer you a drink? Water? I'm afraid I don't have much else."

"Water would be great." Beck looked around the cozy living space. Small, square windows high along one wall allowed for natural sunlight and air but were too far up the wall to provide a view of anything other than blue sky.

Faith handed Beck a glass of water and seemed in no hurry to pull her hand away. Their fingers brushed against each other, and a small jolt traveled up Beck's arm. She was trying to mask her desire for Faith, but she wasn't sure she was succeeding.

"What happens now?" asked Faith.

The thought of evacuating the entire compound had occurred to Beck. She had encouraged Leland to take everyone from the settlement into custody. She wanted to interrogate each person about his or her involvement with the planned bombing. Leland suspected that Meredith and Quinn had acted without Maxine's knowledge, but Beck wasn't convinced.

"Some of the residents want to stay. I think others would like the opportunity to move back to their former urban communities."

"I'll speak to Leland. She'll be the one to decide what happens next." At least some members of the movement had been involved in planning a terrorist bombing, maybe more than one. There would be an investigation and trials. Sorting everything out would likely take months. Initial intel from Leland indicated the Return to Earth movement was splintered ideologically. It was still unclear to Beck how bombing Easton would have served their cause.

"I think Leland wants Maxine to travel back to Paris with us." Beck sipped the water. "A security team will arrive here shortly to set up for questioning the residents. Including you, I'm afraid."

"I understand. Most of us did not support Meredith's actions. We simply want a change. We want the freedom to live where we choose."

It was hard to see Faith as a terrorist. She couldn't. The whole notion of it seemed completely incongruent. Maybe the insurgents had been partly right all along. Maybe she'd fallen prey to the propaganda that humans could only inhabit the cloud cities just like everyone else. A hundred years of separation had shored up the perception that living on the ground was impossible and that anyone who'd remained on the surface when the cities had risen was viewed as lesser, contaminated in some way. This community had been on the ground for ten years according to Leland, and clearly they weren't sick. Beck knew Faith was waiting for her to say more; she could see it in the searching expression on her face.

"Faith, I—" Her throat was dry so she took a sip of water. "I never expected to find you here."

"And I didn't expect to be found." Faith smiled. "But fate seems to have had other ideas."

"Maybe." Beck had never believed in fate, but maybe now was the time to start.

"Beck, you look good. Would it be a bad thing if I confided that I've missed you?"

"No, that wouldn't be bad." Beck's voice was barely above a whisper.

Faith was standing so close. Too close. Beck closed her eyes in an attempt to settle herself. She kept them closed when she felt Faith's lips press lightly against hers. If she opened them, would Faith still be there?

She ran her free hand through Faith's hair, settling it at the back of her neck. Beck applied the slightest bit of pressure to deepen their kiss.

"Faith."

"Beck, I know that I was always the one who wanted to process everything to death. I know I tortured you by wanting to talk through every emotion that passed between us, but I've grown. And I've come to the conclusion that talking is overrated."

Beck smiled. "I've grown too. I've discovered I'm not always right."

Faith laughed.

Beck set the water on a nearby table so that she could hold Faith. She pulled her close. "Faith, I've missed you so much. I failed to cherish what we had, and I've regretted it ever since."

"We both share the blame for letting the end happen."

Beck held Faith's face in both hands and feathered kisses on her forehead, on her cheeks, and then softly kissed her mouth. Their bodies were pressed together as Beck's hands drifted down to Faith's waist. "I'm sorry."

"I'm sorry, too."

"Can we just start over?" Beck studied Faith's soft, bottomless dark eyes for a sign.

"I think we just did."

CHAPTER FORTY

Ava shifted in bed. She wasn't sure what time it was, but bright squares of sunlight lit the dusty floor of her room. They'd gotten back to the compound late the previous evening. The community doctor had tended to the various cuts and scrapes she suffered upon impact. Her left temple ached from the blow against the rock, but still she felt lucky. The rock had caught the cables of the chute and likely kept her from being dragged even farther. She touched the bandage just to remind herself that it was still there.

She moved gingerly to the small bathroom to brush her teeth and wash her face.

After several hours alone in the desert, she was still suffering the effects of dehydration. She couldn't seem to get enough water, but she knew that would pass also. She'd grounded the aircraft and detonated the bomb in a dead zone. All in all, her plan had worked. Except for the part where Leland was gone and she was alone.

Lying in bed, she'd replayed their last conversation in a horrible loop inside her head until exhaustion had finally made sleep possible. She guessed that Beck and Jenna would return for Quinn at any time. She'd hitch a ride with them back to wherever Leland was and do her best to apologize.

She'd lashed out at Leland so unfairly. Ava hated her incendiary temper.

She returned to the main room towel drying her face. Someone knocked softly.

Ava's stomach fluttered and then dropped when she saw Leland standing on the threshold. "You're here."

"I needed to see you. May I come in?"

Leland seemed oddly reserved. Maybe because the last time they'd spoken Ava had been volatile and accusatory. Ava had lashed out because of her own panic and distrust, not because she truly believed she'd been belittled or patronized by Leland. She regretted it all and wished she could take her angry words back.

Ava didn't know how to get them back to where they were before the argument, but she desperately wanted to. She motioned for Leland to come in. As Leland walked past her, she could see the stress on Leland's face. She looked sad, and dark circles under her eyes seemed to emphasize the sadness.

"How is your father?" Ava closed the door softly. She was sure her hair was a mess, and she was still wearing the T-shirt she'd slept in. She figured that to Leland she probably looked worse than she felt.

"He passed away." Leland cleared her throat and turned to face Ava. "He died within an hour of my arrival in CC Easton."

"I'm so sorry."

Leland shook her head and looked at the floor. The melancholy that seemed to envelop Leland was so uncharacteristic that it tightened Ava's stomach into a knot. Was this because of her father's death or was this her fault? Maybe both. Probably both.

"I didn't want to leave until I was sure that you were safe, Ava. I hope you realize that. But Beck insisted that the situation with my father was dire, and in the end, she'd been right."

"I'm so sorry I wasn't there for you." Words were failing Ava. What comfort could she really offer? Grief was something she didn't have a lot of experience with. Saying sorry seemed inadequate, but she wasn't sure what else to say.

"Ava—" Leland couldn't finish whatever she was about to say. Her words seemed to catch in her throat.

Ava took a few steps toward where Leland was standing in the middle of the room. She'd fought the impulse to reach for Leland the minute she'd seen her, but she didn't think she could stand it much longer. Leland seemed so changed. Ava wondered now if she'd ruined everything for them. It didn't matter. She wanted to hold Leland.

She reached for Leland and, for the first time since she'd arrived, Leland looked directly at Ava. The hurt in her eyes was like a punch in the throat.

"Leland, I—" Emotion choked Ava's voice. "Leland, I'm so sorry for everything I said to you when we last spoke. None of it was true. It was all just fear on my part because of the way I was feeling about you and I took it all out on you. That wasn't fair, and I've regretted every word. If I could take it back, I would." The words came out in a rush. Ava felt she couldn't say them fast enough, and she wanted to get all of them out before Leland stopped her.

"Really?" Leland looked hopeful. "I thought you hated me."

Ava shook her head. "The exact opposite is true."

Leland felt a huge sense of relief. She'd been a tangled mess of nerves during the flight back to the desert. She had no idea how Ava felt about her, and she was so afraid that whatever they'd had together was over. What did it matter if she'd inherited the entire world but lost the woman she loved?

It seemed that now there might be a reason to hope they could work something out. Leland wanted so badly to work something out with Ava. She didn't want to go back to a life without her in it. Leland wanted desperately to touch Ava. She wanted to hold her, and she wanted to be held, but both of Ava's arms were covered at least partially with gauze bandages and she also had a bandage on the side of her head.

Leland tentatively reached out but then hesitated, her hand poised in midair. "Ava, are you hurt badly?"

"No, my hard head broke my fall." Ava smiled. "And these are just scrapes. It all looks worse than it is." She moved her arms to show off the bandages.

"Can I…can I hold you?"

Ava didn't answer. She simply reached out for Leland. The sensation of Ava's body cradled against hers was incredibly soothing. Ava's lips brushed her cheek. She shifted in Ava's arms so that their lips met. Lightly, tenderly, they kissed.

"Leland, I love you."

The words she never thought she'd hear Ava say, though uttered softly, reverberated loudly inside her head. "Oh, Ava, I love you, too. So much it hurts. I was so afraid I'd lost you."

They kissed standing in each other's arms in the center of the room, for several minutes. The whole encounter was like a dream sequence for Leland. She finally released Ava and took a step back.

"Leland, I'm so sorry you had to go through losing your father without me there. I wanted to be there for you."

"Maybe it's best you weren't." Leland ran her fingers through her hair. "There were things I needed to face by myself." She brushed a tear away from her cheek. "It's an odd sensation to feel utterly alone. Even though my father and I were distant, he was still an anchor for my world. Without him, well, things feel different. I'm not sure how to explain it."

"I'm here for you now. I'm not going to let you down again."

"You didn't let me down, Ava. I think you saved me."

Ava placed her open palm in the center of Leland's chest. "No, Leland, you saved me."

"Maybe we saved each other."

"Maybe we did." Ava smiled. "So, you're the chancellor now." It was a statement, not a question.

"The ceremony took place within hours of my father's death. Then I flew to Paris to organize a few things. But I wanted to get back here as soon as possible to make sure you were all right."

"What does all this mean?" Ava tilted her head as she studied Leland's face. "What happens now?"

"I was hoping you'd help me change the world."

Ava's eyes widened. "Of course, with enthusiasm, but before we start a revolution, can we get some food?"

Leland laughed. For the first time in days, she genuinely laughed. "I don't suppose you know what time it is? I only just woke up right before you knocked and I'm starving."

Leland pulled out the pocket watch, and Ava couldn't help but smile at the sight of it. "Seeing this reminds me, there's someone I want you to meet before we go back to the city."

"Does this mean you'll come back to Paris with me?"

"Yes, Paris or anywhere. I want to be wherever you are. Didn't you have this whole romantic second date scenario planned for us?" Ava draped her arms lightly around Leland's neck.

"Yes...Yes, I did." Leland glanced down at the watch in her open palm. "By the way, it's two o'clock. You've missed breakfast and lunch." Leland closed the watch and shoved it back in her pocket.

"I suppose dinner might have to wait too." Ava smiled against Leland's lips just before she kissed her.

"Oh, Ava. No one has ever made me feel the way you do. I don't know if this makes sense, but when I'm with you, I feel complete."

"I think I know exactly what you mean."

CHAPTER FORTY-ONE

A va settled back in her seat. It felt good to be in the pilot's chair after being grounded against her will.

Ava looked over and smiled at Leland in the copilot's seat. She only needed one hand on the navigation stick so she entwined her fingers with Leland's across the small console that separated them. They'd replaced the garish gauze bindings on her arms and head with second skin bandages so that Ava looked less injured.

Ava couldn't believe she'd been able to convince Beck to let them fly to Cole's place in the mountains alone.

After everything that had happened, she wasn't sure Beck would ever let Leland out of her sight. But Leland and Ava both knew that once they returned to Paris, Leland's life would be on permanent display. This was their last and only chance to make this journey without an entourage. Beck had argued that she should travel with them, but Ava had assured her Leland had nothing to fear in the mountains. That Leland would find only friendship there, as she had so many months ago.

Ava actually thought Faith might thank her upon their return because it seemed that Faith wanted Beck to herself for a little while. In light of that, Beck might also be grateful.

"How do you like the copilot's chair?" Ava asked.

"I like it. I might be ruined now for sitting in the passenger compartment."

They sat in silence and then Ava had a thought that made her laugh.

"What's funny?" asked Leland.

"I was just thinking that in the past year I had to make an emergency landing in the mountains, I nearly crashed due to an injury, and then a plane I was flying was forced down by a hijacker." Ava shook her head. "I'm either the worst pilot ever or just the most unlucky."

"You're still alive. Maybe that makes you the best pilot ever." Leland squeezed her hand. "Or maybe just the luckiest."

Ava looked over at Leland. "Definitely the luckiest." She raised Leland's fingers to her lips and kissed them.

They'd left the desert early and would be touching down in the Blue Mountains in a matter of minutes. Ava was nervous and calm at the same time. Nervous about seeing Cole and Audrey, but at the same time calm because she knew they'd love Leland just as much as she did.

She initiated their descent and banked the plane as they flew over the tall golden grass in the field beneath them, the golden grass that Ava had seen so long ago in her dreams. She circled once and landed the cruiser at the end of the pasture closest to Cole's family cabin.

Ava didn't know who would be on the property when they arrived, and she hoped she could remember the way. When she was last in this place, Cole had moved into a dwelling of her own, and only her aunts, Vivian and Ida, kept their residence in the cabin.

Once they'd climbed out of the aircraft, Ava felt a surge of familiarity. She did know the way, and she tugged Leland by the hand toward the trail through the woods. As they walked Leland asked questions about what she was seeing. The foliage and topography was so different from the desert that Ava knew Leland would be mesmerized by it all. She tried her best to recall things from memory, but she knew Cole would be able to give Leland a much better guided tour than she could.

"I wanted you to see this place, Leland. I wanted you to experience the community here on the ground. A community where people are happy. Where they have a good life."

"Thank you for bringing me here, Ava."

"If you really want to change the world, it's good to get a glimpse of this side of it. It's very different here in almost every way from what we just experienced in the desert. And from what life is like in the cities."

As they neared the clearing around the cabin, Ava felt her pulse quicken. She turned and gave Leland a reassuring smile. As she stepped from the tree line, Ava saw that Cole was leaning against one of the porch railings looking in her direction. She watched from across the lawn as the expression on Cole's face shifted to shock and then settled again into a broad grin.

"Ava!" Cole turned back and yelled into the open front door of the cabin. "Ava is here!" She trotted down the steps and met them as they crossed the yard.

"That's Cole." Ava dropped Leland's hand and increased her pace in Cole's direction.

Leland watched Cole approach. She was tall and thin, with a boyish sort of build, and short dark hair that fell haphazardly across her forehead. Cole swept Ava up in her arms and twirled her around.

Leland watched the reunion between Ava and Cole. Then three other women spilled out of the cabin and headed in their direction. Based on Ava's previous descriptions, she knew one of them was Audrey. She was beautiful, with long wavy auburn hair falling past her shoulders. She exuded affection as she joined Cole in embracing Ava.

"Hello, I'm Vivian. Welcome." A woman, probably in her fifties, tall and leanly muscled with angular features and short dark hair extended her hand to Leland.

"Hello, so nice to meet you. I'm Leland."

"And I'm Cole's aunt, Ida." Where Vivian was tall and lean, Ida was softer, with gray hair pulled back into a loose knot that allowed wisps of it to break free and frame her smiling face.

Cole and Audrey finally released Ava. Then Ida and Vivian were next, wrapping Ava in an affectionate embrace. Ida fussed about the bandages, but Ava assured her that she was well.

Leland, Cole, and Audrey introduced themselves. Leland wasn't sure what she'd expected, but the warmth and joy emanating from these four women was contagious. She felt lifted up by them. She felt renewed.

Ava reached for Leland's hand and pulled her close. "Everyone, this is Leland Argosy. I'm sorry to show up without some advance warning, but I really wanted all of you to meet."

"Leland must be a very special person." Audrey smiled as if she truly understood what Ava was trying to communicate by bringing Leland to meet them.

"She is." Ava felt heat rise to her cheeks. She rarely blushed, but under Audrey's playful scrutiny was certain she probably was. Ava felt almost as if she were bringing her fiancé home to meet her chosen family. Upon brief reflection, Ava supposed that was exactly what she was doing.

"Well, girls, we were just about to have some lunch. Please, let's go in the house." Ida started herding the group toward the porch. "Ava, you can eat and fill us in on your life. It's been months since we've seen you and you look too thin!" Then Ida put an arm around Leland's waist in a maternal fashion. "And, Leland, we don't know you at all. You'll have to tell us all about yourself."

Ida and Vivian ushered Leland into the house. Audrey followed on their heels.

"Ava, it's so good to see you." Cole squeezed her shoulders and then followed the others up the steps while Ava lingered in the grass near the bottom step.

She spun in a slow circle breathing in the scent of hardwoods, grass, and the Earth itself.

What did it mean to change the world?

Ava realized that every revolution probably started small, maybe with nothing more than a vague sense of restless longing.

As she stepped up onto the porch to follow the others into the warm interior of the rustic cabin, Ava realized her world had already shifted on its axis.

Ava trusted for the first time in someone other than herself. With Leland, she sincerely believed anything was possible, even changing the world. Because once you feel changed, transformed even, possibilities seem limitless.

The End

About the Author

Missouri Vaun spent most of her childhood in rural southern Mississippi, where she spent lazy summers conjuring characters and imagining the worlds they might inhabit. Missouri spent twelve years finding her voice as a working journalist in places as disparate as Chicago and Jackson, Mississippi. Her stories are heartfelt, earthy, and speak of loyalty and our responsibility to others. She and her wife currently live in northern California. Missouri can be reached via email at: Missouri.Vaun@gmail.com or via the Web at: MissouriVaun.com.

Books Available from Bold Strokes Books

Camp Rewind by Meghan O'Brien. A summer camp for grown-ups becomes the site of an unlikely romance between a shy, introverted divorcee and one of the Internet's most infamous cultural critics—who attends undercover. (978-1-62639-793-4)

Cross Purposes by Gina L. Dartt. In pursuit of a lost Acadian treasure, three women must not only work out the clues, but also the complicated tangle of emotion and attraction developing between them. (978-1-62639-713-2)

Imperfect Truth by C.A. Popovich. Can an imperfect truth stand in the way of love? (978-1-62639-787-3)

Life in Death by M. Ullrich. Sometimes the devastating end is your only chance for a new beginning. (978-1-62639-773-6)

Love on Liberty by MJ Williamz. Hearts collide when politics clash. (978-1-62639-639-5)

Serious Potential by Maggie Cummings. Pro golfer Tracy Allen plans to forget her ex during a visit to Bay West, a lesbian condo community in NYC, but when she meets Dr. Jennifer Betsy, she gets more than she bargained for. (978-1-62639-633-3)

Taste by Kris Bryant. Accomplished chef Taryn has walked away from her promising career in the city's top restaurant to devote her life to her five-year-old daughter and is content until Ki Blake comes along. (978-1-62639-718-7)

The Second Wave by Jean Copeland. Can star-crossed lovers have a second chance after decades apart, or does the love of a lifetime only happen once? (978-1-62639-830-6)

Valley of Fire by Missouri Vaun. Taken captive in a desert outpost after their small aircraft is hijacked, Ava and her captivating passenger discover things about each other and themselves that will change them both forever. (978-1-62639-496-4)

Basic Training of the Heart by Jaycie Morrison. In 1944, socialite Elizabeth Carlton joins the Women's Army Corps to escape family expectations and love's disappointments. Can Sergeant Gale Rains get her through Basic Training with their hearts intact? (978-1-62639-818-4)

Before by KE Payne. When Tally falls in love with her band's new recruit, she has a tough decision to make. What does she want more—Alex or the band? (978-1-62639-677-7)

Believing in Blue by Maggie Morton. Growing up gay in a small town has been hard, but it can't compare to the next challenge Wren—with her new, sky-blue wings—faces: saving two entire worlds. (978-1-62639-691-3)

Coils by Barbara Ann Wright. A modern young woman follows her aunt into the Greek Underworld and makes a pact with Medusa to win her freedom by killing a hero of legend. (978-1-62639-598-5)

Courting the Countess by Jenny Frame. When relationship-phobic Lady Henrietta Knight starts to care about housekeeper Annie Brannigan and her daughter, can she overcome her fears and promise Annie the forever that she demands? (978-1-62639-785-9)

Dapper by Jenny Frame. Amelia Honey meets the mysterious Byron De Brek and is faced with her darkest fantasies, but will her strict moral upbringing stop her from exploring what she truly wants? (978-1-62639-898-6E)

Delayed Gratification: The Honeymoon by Meghan O'Brien. A dream European honeymoon turns into a winter storm nightmare involving a delayed flight, a ditched rental car, and eventually, a surprisingly happy ending. (978-1-62639-766-8E)

For Money or Love by Heather Blackmore. Jessica Spaulding must choose between ignoring the truth to keep everything she has, and doing the right thing only to lose it all—including the woman she loves. (978-1-62639-756-9)

Hooked by Jaime Maddox. With the help of sexy Detective Mac Calabrese, Dr. Jessica Benson is working hard to overcome her past, but it may not be enough to stop a murderer. (978-1-62639-689-0)

Lands End by Jackie D. Public relations superstar Amy Kline is dealing with a media nightmare, and the last thing she expects is for restaurateur Lena Michaels to change everything, but she will. (978-1-62639-739-2)

Lysistrata Cove by Dena Hankins. Jack and Eve navigate the maelstrom of their darkest desires and find love by transgressing gender, dominance, submission, and the law on the crystal blue Caribbean Sea. (978-1-62639-821-4)

Twisted Screams by Sheri Lewis Wohl. Reluctant psychic Lorna Dutton doesn't want to forgive, but if she doesn't do just that an innocent woman will die. (978-1-62639-647-0)

A Class Act by Tammy Hayes. Buttoned-up college professor Dr. Margaret Parks doesn't know what she's getting herself into when she agrees to one date with her student, Rory Morgan, who is 15 years her junior. (978-1-62639-701-9)

Bitter Root by Laydin Michaels. Small town chef Adi Bergeron is hiding something, and Griffith McNaulty is going to find out what it is even if it gets her killed. (978-1-62639-656-2)

Capturing Forever by Erin Dutton. When family pulls Jacqueline and Casey back together, will the lessons learned in eight years apart be enough to mend the mistakes of the past? (978-1-62639-631-9)

Deception by VK Powell. DEA Agent Colby Vincent and Attorney Adena Weber are embroiled in a drug investigation involving homeless veterans and an attraction that could destroy them both. (978-1-62639-596-1)

Dyre: A Knight of Spirit and Shadows by Rachel E. Bailey. With the abduction of her queen, werewolf-bodyguard Des must follow the kidnappers' trail to Europe, where her queen—and a battle unlike any Des has ever waged—awaits her. (978-1-62639-664-7)

First Position by Melissa Brayden. Love and rivalry take center stage for Anastasia Mikhelson and Natalie Frederico in one of the most prestigious ballet companies in the nation. (978-1-62639-602-9)

Best Laid Plans by Jan Gayle. Nicky and Lauren are meant for each other, but Nicky's haunting past and Lauren's societal fears threaten to derail all possibilities of a relationship. (987-1-62639-658-6)

Exchange by CF Frizzell. When Shay Maguire rode into rural Montana, she never expected to meet the woman of her dreams—or to learn Mel Baker was held hostage by legal agreement to her right-wing father. (987-1-62639-679-1)

Just Enough Light by AJ Quinn. Will a serial killer's return to Colorado destroy Kellen Ryan and Dana Kingston's chance at love, or can the search-and-rescue team save themselves? (987-1-62639-685-2)

Rise of the Rain Queen by Fiona Zedde. Nyandoro is nobody's princess. She fights, curses, fornicates, and gets into as much trouble as her brothers. But the path to a throne is not always the one we expect. (987-1-62639-592-3)

Tales from Sea Glass Inn by Karis Walsh. Over the course of a year at Cannon Beach, tourists and locals alike find solace and passion at the Sea Glass Inn. (987-1-62639-643-2)

The Color of Love by Radclyffe. Black sheep Derian Winfield needs to convince literary agent Emily May to marry her to save the Winfield Agency and solve Emily's green card problem, but Derian didn't count on falling in love. (987-1-62639-716-3)

A Reluctant Enterprise by Gun Brooke. When two women grow up learning nothing but distrust, unworthiness, and abandonment, it's no wonder they are apprehensive and fearful when an overwhelming love just won't be denied. (978-1-62639-500-8)

Above the Law by Carsen Taite. Love is the last thing on Agent Dale Nelson's mind, but reporter Lindsey Ryan's investigation could change the way she sees everything—her career, her past, and her future. (978-1-62639-558-9)

Jane's World: The Case of the Mail Order Bride by Paige Braddock. Jane's PayBuddy account gets hacked and she inadvertently purchases a mail order bride from the Eastern Bloc. (978-1-62639-494-0)

Love's Redemption by Donna K. Ford. For ex-convict Rhea Daniels and ex-priest Morgan Scott, redemption lies in the thin line between right and wrong. (978-1-62639-673-9)

The Shewstone by Jane Fletcher. The prophetic Shewstone is in Eawynn's care, but unfortunately for her, Matt is coming to steal it. (978-1-62639-554-1)